When Patty
Went To College

Jean Webster

(Illustrated by C. D. Williams)

CONTENTS

LIST OF ILLUSTRATIONS

TO 234 MAIN AND THE GOOD TIMES WE HAVE HAD THERE

I Peters the Susceptible

PAPER-WEIGHTS," observed Patty, sucking an injured thumb, "were evidently not made for driving in tacks. I wish I had a hammer."

This remark called forth no response, and Patty peered down from the top of the step-ladder at her room-mate, who was sitting on the floor dragging sofa-pillows and curtains from a dry-goods box.

"Priscilla," she begged, "you are n't doing anything useful. Go down and ask Peters for a hammer."

Priscilla rose reluctantly. "I dare say fifty girls have already been after a hammer."

"Oh, he has a private one in his back pocket. Borrow that. And, Pris,"–Patty called after her over the transom,–"just tell him to send up a man to take that closet door off its hinges."

Patty, in the interval, sat down on the top step and surveyed the chaos beneath her. An Oriental rush chair, very much out at the elbows, several miscellaneous chairs, two desks, a divan, a table, and two dry-goods boxes radiated from the center of the room. The floor, as it showed through the interstices, was covered with a grass-green carpet, while the curtains and hangings were of a not very subdued crimson.

"One would scarcely," Patty remarked to the furniture in general, "call it a symphony in color."

A knock sounded on the door.

"Come in," she called.

A girl in a blue linen sailor-suit reaching to her ankles, and with a braid of hair hanging down her back, appeared in the doorway. Patty examined her in silence. The girl's eyes traveled around the room in some surprise, and finally reached the top of the ladder.

"I–I 'm a freshman," she began.

"My dear," murmured Patty, in a deprecatory tone, "I should have taken you for a senior; but"–with a wave of her hand toward the nearest dry-goods box–"come in and sit down. I need your advice. Now, there are shades of green," she went on, as if continuing a conversation, "which are not so bad with red; but I ask you frankly if that shade of green would go with anything?"

The freshman looked at Patty, and looked at the carpet. and smiled dubiously. "No," she admitted; "I don't believe it would."

"I knew you would say that!" exclaimed Patty, in a tone of relief. "Now what would you advise us to do with the carpet?"

The freshman looked blank. "I–I don't know, unless you take it up," she stammered.

"The very thing!" said Patty. "I wonder we had n't thought of it before."

Priscilla reappeared at this point with the announcement, "Peters is the most suspicious man I ever knew!" But she stopped uncertainly as she caught sight of the freshman.

"Priscilla," said Patty, severely, "I hope you did n't divulge the fact that we are hanging the walls with tapestry"–this with a wave of her hand toward the printed cotton cloth dangling from the molding.

"I tried not to," said Priscilla, guiltily, "but he read 'tapestry' in my eyes. He had no sooner looked at me than he said, 'See here, miss; you know it 's against the rules to hang curtains on the walls, and you must n't put nails in the plastering, and I don't believe you need a hammer anyway,'"

"Disgusting creature!" said Patty.

"But," continued Priscilla, hastily, "I stopped and borrowed Georgie Merriles's hammer on my way back. Oh, I forgot," she added; "he says we can't take the closet door off its hinges–that as soon as we get ours off five hundred other young ladies will be wanting theirs off, and that it would take half a dozen men all summer to put them back again."

2

A portentous frown was gathering on Patty's brow, and the freshman, wishing to avert a possible domestic tragedy, inquired timidly, "Who is Peters?"

"Peters," said Priscilla, "is a short, bow-legged gentleman with a red Vandyke beard, whose technical title is janitor, but who is really dictator. Every one is afraid of him–even Prexy."

"I 'm not," said Patty; "and," she added firmly, "that door is coming down whether he says so or not, so I suppose we shall have to do it ourselves." Her eyes wandered back to the carpet and her face brightened. "Oh, Pris, we 've got a beautiful new scheme. My friend here says she does n't like the carpet at all, and suggests that we take it up, get some black paint, and put it on the floor ourselves. I agree," she added, "that a Flemish oak floor covered with rugs would be a great improvement."

Priscilla glanced uncertainly from the freshman to the floor. "Do you think they 'd let us do it?"

"It would never do to ask them," said Patty.

The freshman rose uneasily. "I came," she said hesitatingly, "to find out–that is, I understand that the girls rent their old books, and I thought, if you would n't mind–"

"Mind!" said Patty, reassuringly. "We 'd rent our souls for fifty cents a semester."

"It–it was a Latin dictionary I wanted," said the freshman, "and the girls next door said perhaps you had one."

"A beautiful one," said Patty.

" No," interrupted Priscilla "hers is lost from O to R, and it 's all torn; but mine,"–she dived down into one of the boxes and hauled out a chunky volume without any covers,–"while it is not so beautiful as it was once, it is still as useful."

"Mine 's annotated," said Patty, "and illustrated. I 'll show you what a superior book it is," and she began descending the ladder; but Priscilla charged upon her and she retreated to the top again. "Why," she wailed to the terrified freshman, "did you not say you wanted a dictionary before she came back? Let me give you some advice at the beginning of your college career," she added warningly. "Never choose a room-mate bigger than yourself. They 're dangerous."

The freshman was backing precipitously toward the door, when it opened and revealed an attractive-looking girl with fluffy reddish hair.

"Pris, you wretch, you walked off with my hammer!"

"Oh, Georgie, we need it worse than you do! Come in and help tack."

"Hello, Georgie," called Patty, from the ladder. "Is n't this room going to be beautiful when it 's finished?"

Georgie looked about. "You are more sanguine than I should be," she laughed.

"You can't tell yet," Patty returned. "We 're going to cover the wall-paper with this red stuff, and paint the floor black, and have dark furniture, and red hangings, and soft lights. It will look just like the Oriental Room in the Waldorf."

"How in the world," Georgie demanded, "do you ever make them let you do all these things? I stuck in three innocent little thumb-tacks to-day, and Peters descended upon me bristling with wrath, and said he 'd report me if I did n't pull them out."

"We never ask," explained Patty. "It 's the only way."

"You 've got enough to do if you expect to get settled by Monday," Georgie remarked.

"C'est vrai," agreed Patty, descending the ladder with a sudden access of energy; "and you 've got to stay and help us. We have to get all this furniture moved into the bedrooms and the carpet up before we even begin to paint." She regarded the freshman tentatively. "Are you awfully busy?"

"Not very. My room-mate has n't come yet, so I can't settle."

"That 's nice; then you can help us move furniture."

"Patty!" said Priscilla, "I think you are too bad."

"I should really love to stay and help, if you 'll let me."

"Certainly," said Patty, obligingly. "I forgot to ask your name," she continued, "and I don't suppose you like to be called 'Freshman'; it 's not specific enough."

"My name is Genevieve Ainslee Randolph."

"Genevieve Ains–dear me! I can't remember anything like that. Do you mind if I call you Lady Clara Vere de Vere for short?"

The freshman looked doubtful, and Patty proceeded: "Lady Clara, allow me to present my room-mate Miss Priscilla Pond–no relation to the extract. She 's athletic and wins hundred-yard dashes and hurdle races, and gets her name in the paper to a really gratifying extent. And my dear friend Miss Georgie Merriles, one of the oldest families in Dakota. Miss Merriles is very talented–sings in the glee club, plays on the comb–"

"And," interrupted Georgie, "let me present Miss Patty Wyatt, who–"

"Has no specialty," said Patty, modestly, "but is merely good and beautiful and bright."

A knock sounded on the door, which opened without waiting for a response. "Miss Theodora Bartlet," continued Patty, "commonly known as the Twin, Miss Vere de Vere."

The Twin looked dazed, murmured, "Miss Vere de Vere," and dropped down on a dry-goods box.

"The term 'Twin,'" explained Patty, "is used in a merely allegorical sense. There is really only one of her. The title was conferred in her freshman year, and the reason has been lost in the dim dawn of antiquity."

The freshman looked at the Twin and opened her mouth, but shut it again without saying anything.

"My favorite maxim," said Patty, "has always been, 'Silence is golden.' I observe that we are kindred spirits."

"Patty," said Priscilla, "do stop bothering that poor child and get to work."

"Bothering?" said Patty. "I am not bothering her; we are just getting acquainted. However, I dare say it is not the time for hollow civilities. Do you want to borrow anything?" she added, turning to the Twin, "or did you just drop in to pay a social call?"

"Just a social call; but I think I 'll come in again when there 's no furniture to move."

"You don't happen to be going into town this afternoon?"

"Yes," said the Twin. "But," she added guardedly, "if it 's a curtain-pole, I refuse to bring it out. I offered to bring one out for Lucille Carter last night, because she was in a hurry to give a house-warming, and I speared the conductor with it getting into the car; and while I was apologizing to him I knocked Mrs. Prexy's hat off with the other end."

"We have all the curtain-poles we need," said Patty. "It 's just some paint–five cans of black paint, and three brushes at the ten-cent store, and thank you very much. Good-by. Now," she continued, "the first thing is to get that door down, and I will wrest a screw-driver from the unwilling Peters while you remove tacks from the carpet."

"He won't give you one," said Priscilla.

"You 'll see," said Patty.

Five minutes later she returned waving above her head an unmistakable screw-driver. "Voilà, mes amies! Peters's own private screw-driver, for which I am to be personally responsible."

"How did you get it?" inquired Priscilla, suspiciously.

"You act," said Patty, "as if you thought I knocked him down in some dark corner and robbed him. I merely asked him for it politely, and he asked me what I wanted to do with it. I told him I wanted to take out screws, and the reason impressed him so that he handed it over without a word. Peters," she added, "is a dear; only he 's like every other man–you have to use diplomacy."

By ten o'clock that night the study carpet of 399 was neatly folded and deposited at the end of the corridor above, whence its origin would be difficult to trace. The entire region was steeped in an odor of turpentine, and the study floor of 399 was a shining black, except for four or five unpainted spots which Patty designated as "stepping-stones," and which were to be treated later. Every caller that had dropped in during the afternoon or evening had had a brush thrust into her hand and had been made to go down upon her knees and paint. Besides the floor, three bookcases and a chair had been transferred from mahogany to Flemish oak, and there was still half a can of paint left which Patty was anxiously trying to dispose of.

The next morning, in spite of the difficulty of getting about, the step-ladder had been reërected, and the business of tapestry-hanging was going forward with enthusiasm, when a knock suddenly interrupted the work.

Patty, all unconscious of impending doom, cheerily called, "Come in!"

The door opened, and the figure of Peters appeared on the threshold; and Priscilla basely fled, leaving her room-mate stranded on the ladder.

"Are you the young lady who borrowed my screw–" Peters stopped and looked at the floor, and his jaw dropped in astonishment. "Where is that there carpet?" he demanded, in a tone which seemed to imply that he thought it was under the paint.

"It 's out in the hall," said Patty, pleasantly. "Please be careful and don't step on the paint. It 's a great improvement, don't you think?"

"You oughter got permission–" he began, but his eye fell on the tapestry and he stopped again.

"Yes," said Patty; "but we knew you could n't spare a man just now to paint it for us, so we did n't like to trouble you."

Men know such a lot about such things!

"It 's against the rules to hang curtains on the walls."

"I have heard that it was," said Patty, affably, "and I think ordinarily it 's a very good rule. But just look at the color of that wall-paper. It 's pea-green. You have had enough experience with wall-paper, Mr. Peters, to know that that is impossible, especially when our window-curtains and portières are red."

Peters's eyes had traveled to the closet, bereft of its door. "Are you the young lady," he demanded gruffly, "who asked me to have that door taken off its hinges?"

"No," said Patty; "I think that must have been my room-mate. It was very heavy," she continued plaintively, "and we had a great deal of trouble getting it down, but of course we realized that you were awfully busy, and that it really was n't your fault. That 's what I wanted the screw-driver for," she added. "I 'm sorry that I did n't get it back last night, but I was very tired, and I forgot."

Peters merely grunted. He was examining a corner cabinet hanging on the wall. "Did n't you know," he asked severely, "that it 's against the rules to put nails in the plaster?"

"Those are n't nails," expostulated Patty. "They 're hooks. I remembered that you did n't like holes, so I only put in two, though I am really afraid that three are necessary. What do you think, Mr. Peters? Does it seem solid?"

Peters shook it. "It 's solid enough," he said sulkily. As he turned, his eye fell on the table in Priscilla's bedroom. "Is that a gas-stove in there?" he demanded.

Patty shrugged her shoulders. "An apology for one–be careful, Mr. Peters! Don't get against that bookcase. It 's just painted."

Peters jumped aside, and stood like the Colossus of Rhodes, with one foot on one stepping-stone, and the other on another three feet away. It is hard for even a janitor to be dignified in such a position, and while he was gathering his scattered impressions Patty looked longingly around the room for some one to enjoy the spectacle with her. She felt that the silence was becoming ominous, however, and she hastened to interrupt it.

"There 's something wrong with that stove; it won't burn a bit. I am afraid we did n't put it together just right. I should n't be surprised if you might be able to tell what 's the matter with it, Mr. Peters." She smiled sweetly. "Men know such a lot about such things! Would you mind looking at it?"

Peters grunted again; but he approached the stove.

Five minutes later, when Priscilla stuck her head in to find out if, by chance, anything remained of Patty, she saw Peters on his knees on the floor of her bedroom, with the dismembered stove scattered about him, and heard him saying, "I don't know as I have any call to report you, for I s'pose, since they 're up, they might as well stay"; and Patty's voice returning: "You 're very kind, Mr. Peters. Of course if we 'd known–" Priscilla shut the door softly, and retired around the corner to await Peters's departure.

"How in the world did you manage him?" she asked, bursting in as soon as the sound of his footsteps had died away down the corridor. "I expected to sing a requiem over your remains, and I found Peters on his knees, engaged in amicable conversation."

Patty smiled inscrutably. "You must remember," she said, "that Peters is not only a janitor: he is also a man."

II An Early Fright

I'LL make the tea to-day," said Patty, graciously.

"As you please," said Priscilla, with a skeptical shrug.

Patty bustled about amid a rattle of china. "The cups are rather dusty," she observed dubiously.

"You 'd better wash them," Priscilla returned.

"No," said Patty; "it 's too much trouble. Just close the blinds, please, and we 'll light the candles, and that will do as well. Come in," she called in answer to a knock.

Georgie Merriles, Lucille Carter, and the Bartlet Twin appeared in the doorway.

"Did I hear the two P's were going to serve tea this afternoon?" inquired the Twin.

"Yes; come in. I 'm going to make it myself," answered Patty, "and you 'll see how much more attentive a hostess I am than Priscilla. Here, Twin," she added, "you take the kettle out and fill it with water; and, Lucille, please go and borrow some alcohol from the freshmen at the end of the corridor; our bottle 's empty. I 'd do it myself, only I 've borrowed such a lot lately, and they don't know you, you see. And–oh, Georgie, you 're an obliging dear; just run down-stairs to the store and get some sugar. I think I saw some money in that silver inkstand on Priscilla's desk."

"We 've got some sugar," objected Priscilla. "I bought a whole pound yesterday."

"No, my lamb; we have n't got it any more. I lent it to Bonnie Connaught last night. Just hunt around for the spoons," she added. "I think I saw them on the bottom shelf of the bookcase, behind Kipling."

"And what, may I ask, are you going to do?" inquired Priscilla.

"I?" said Patty. "Oh, I am going to sit in the arm-chair and preside."

Ten minutes later, the company being disposed about the room on cushions, and the party well under way, it was discovered that there were no lemons.

"Are you sure?" asked Patty, anxiously.

"Not one," said Priscilla, peering into the stein where the lemons were kept.

"I," said Georgie, "refuse to go to the store again."

"No matter," said Patty, graciously; "we can do very well without them." (She did not take lemon herself.) "The object of tea is not for the sake of the tea, but for the conversation which accompanies it, and one must not let accidents annoy him. You see, young ladies," she went on, in the tone of an instructor giving a lecture, "though I have just spilled the alcohol over the sugar, I appear not to notice it, but keep up an easy flow of conversation to divert my guests. A repose of manner is above all things to be cultivated." Patty leaned languidly back in her chair. "To-morrow is Founder's Day," she resumed in a conversational tone. "I wonder if many–"

"That reminds me," interrupted the Twin. "You girls need n't save any dances for my brother. I got a letter from him this morning saying he could n't come."

"He has n't broken anything, has he?" Patty asked sympathetically.

"Broken anything?"

"Ah–an arm, or a leg, or a neck. Accidents are so prevalent about Founder's time."

"No; he was called out of town on important business."

"Important business!" Patty laughed. "Dear man! why could n't he have thought of something new?"

"I think myself it was just an excuse," the Twin acknowledged. "He seemed to have an idea that he would be the only man here, and that, alone and unaided, he would have to dance with all six hundred girls."

Patty shook her head sadly. "They 're all alike. Founder's would n't be Founder's if half the guests did n't develop serious illness or important business or dead relations the last minute. The only safe way is to invite three men and make out one program."

"I simply can't realize that to-morrow is Founder's," said Priscilla. "It does n't seem a week since we unpacked our trunks after vacation, and before we know it we shall be packing them again for Christmas."

"Yes; and before we know it we 'll be unpacking them again, with examinations three weeks ahead," said Georgie the pessimist.

"Oh, for the matter of that," returned Patty the optimist, "before we know it we 'll be walking up one side of the platform for our diplomas and coming down the other side blooming alumnæ."

"And then," sighed Georgie, "before we even have time to decide on a career, we 'll be old ladies, telling our grandchildren to stand up straight and remember their rubbers."

"And," said Priscilla, "before any of us get any tea we 'll be in our graves, if you don't stop talking and watch that kettle."

"It 's boiling," said Patty.

"Yes," said Priscilla; "it 's been boiling for ten minutes."

"It 's hot," said Patty.

"I should think it might be," said Priscilla.

"And now the problem is, how to get it off without burning one's self."

"You 're presiding to-day; you must solve your own problems."

"'T is an easy matter," and Patty hooked it off on the end of a golf-club. "Young ladies," she said, with a wave of the kettle, "there is nothing like a college education to teach you a way out of every difficulty. If, when you are out in the wide, wide world–"

"Where, oh, where are the grave old seniors?" chanted the Twin. "Where, oh, where are they?"

The rest took it up, and Patty waited patiently.

"They 've gone out of Cairnsley's ethics, They 've gone out of Cairnsley's ethics, They 've gone out of Cairnsley's ethics, Into the wide, wide w-o-r-1-d." "If you have finished your ovation, young ladies, I will proceed with my lecture. When, as I say, you are out in the wide, wide world, making five-o'clock tea some afternoon for one of the young men popularly supposed to be there, who have dropped in to make an afternoon call– Do you follow me, young ladies, or do I speak too fast? If, while you are engaged in conversation, the kettle should become too hot, do not put your finger in your mouth and shriek 'Ouch!' and coquettishly say to the young man, 'You take it off,' as might a young woman who has not enjoyed your advantages; but, rather, rise to the emergency; say to him calmly, 'This kettle has become over-heated; may I trouble you to go into the hall and bring an umbrella?' and when he returns you can hook it off gracefully and expeditiously as you have seen me do, young ladies, and the young–"

"Patty, take care!" This from Priscilla.

"0-u-c-h!" in along-drawn wail. This from Georgie.

Patty hastily set the kettle down on the floor. "I 'm awfully sorry, Georgie. Does it hurt?"

"Not in the least. It 's really a pleasant sensation to have boiling water poured over you."

The Bartlet Twin sniffed. "I smell burning rug."

Patty groaned. "I resign, Pris; I resign. Here, you preside. I 'll never ask to make it again."

"I should like," observed the Twin, "to see Patty entertaining a young man."

"It 's not such an unprecedented event," said Patty, with some warmth. "You can watch me to-morrow night if it will give you so much pleasure."

"To-morrow night? Are you going to have a man for the Prom?"

"That," said Patty, "is my intention."

"And you have n't asked me for a dance!" This in an aggrieved chorus from the entire room.

"I have n't asked any one," said Patty, with dignity.

"Do you mean you 're going to have all of the twenty dances with him yourself?"

"Oh, no; I don't expect to dance more than ten with him myself–I have n't made out his card yet," she added.

"Why not?"

"I never do."

"Has he been here before, then?"

"No; that 's the reason."

"The reason for what?"

"Well," Patty deigned to explain, "I 've invited him for every party since freshman year."

"And did he decline?"

"No; he accepted, but he never came."

"Why not?"

"He was scared."

"Scared? Of the girls?"

"Yes," said Patty, "partly–but mostly of the faculty."

"The faculty would n't hurt him."

"Of course not; but he could n't understand that. You see, he had a fright when he was young."

"A fright? What was it?"

"Well," said Patty, "it happened this way: It was while I was at boarding-school. He was at Andover then, and his home was in the South; and one time when he went through Washington he stopped off to call on me. As it happened, the butler had left two days before, and had taken with him all the knives and forks, and all the money he could find, and Nancy Lee's gold watch and two hat-pins, and my silver hair-brush, and a bottle of brandy, and a pie," she enumerated with a conscientious regard for details; "and Mrs. Trent–that 's the principal–had advertised for a new butler,"

"I should have thought the old one would have discouraged her from keeping butlers," said Georgie.

"You would think so," said Patty; "but she was a very persevering woman. On the day that Raoul–that 's his name–came to call, nineteen people had applied for the place, and Mrs. Trent was worn out from interviewing them. So she told Miss Sarah–that 's her daughter–to attend to those who came in the evening. Miss Sarah was tall and wore spectacles, and was–was– "

"A good disciplinarian," suggested the Twin.

"Yes," said Patty, feelingly, "an awfully good disciplinarian. Well, when Raoul got there he gave his card to Ellen and asked for me; but Ellen did n't understand, and she called Miss Sarah, and when Miss Sarah saw him in his evening clothes she–"

"Took him for a butler," put in Georgie.

"Yes, she took him for a butler; and she looked at the card he 'd given Ellen, and said icily, 'What does this mean?'

"'It 's–it 's my name,' he stammered.

"'I see,' said Miss Sarah; 'but where is your recommendation?'

16

"'I did n't know it was necessary,' he said, terribly scared.

"'Of course it 's necessary,' Miss Sarah returned. 'I can't allow you to come into the house unless I have letters from the places where you 've been before.'

"'I did n't suppose you were so strict,' he said.

"'We have to be strict,' Miss Sarah answered firmly. 'Have you had much experience?'

"He did n't know what she meant, but he thought it would be safest to say he had n't.

"'Then of course you won't do,' she replied. 'How old are you?'

"'He was so frightened by this time that he could n't remember. 'Nineteen,' he gasped—'I mean twenty.'

"Miss Sarah saw his confusion, and thought he had designs on some of the heiresses intrusted to her care. 'I don't see how you dared to come here,' she said severely. 'I should not think of having you in the house for a moment. You 're altogether too young and too good-looking.' And with that Raoul got up and bolted.

"When Ellen told Miss Sarah the next day that he 'd asked for me, she was terribly mortified, and she made me write and explain, and invite him to dinner; but wild horses could n't have dragged him into the house again. He 's been afraid to stop off in Washington ever since. He always goes straight through on a sleeper, and says he has nightmares even then."

"And is that why he won't come to the college?"

"Yes," said Patty; "that's the reason. I told him we did n't have any butlers here; but he said we had lady faculty, and that 's as bad."

"But I thought you said he was coming to the Prom."

"He is this time."

"Are you sure?"

"Yes," said Patty, with ominous emphasis, "I 'm sure. He knows," she added, "what will happen if he does n't."

"What will happen?" asked the Twin.

"Nothing."

The Twin shook her head, and Georgie inquired, "Then why don't you make out his program?"

"I suppose I might as well. I did n't do it before because it sort of seemed like tempting Providence. I did n't want to be the cause of any really serious accident happening to him," she explained a trifle ambiguously as she got out pencil and paper. "What dances can you give me, Lucille? And you, Georgie, have you got the third taken?"

While this business was being settled, a knock unheeded had sounded on the door. It came again.

"What 's that?" asked Priscilla. "Did some one knock? Come in."

The door opened, and a maid stood upon the threshold with a yellow envelop in her hand. She peered uncertainly around the darkened room from one face to another. "Miss Patty Wyatt?" she asked.

Patty stretched out her hand in silence for the envelop, and, propping it up on her desk, looked at it with a grim smile.

"What is it, Patty? Are n't you going to read it?"

"There 's no need. I know what it says."

"Then I 'll read it," said Priscilla, ripping it open.

"Is it a leg or an arm?" Patty inquired with mild curiosity

"Neither," said Priscilla; "it 's a collar-bone."

"Oh," murmured Patty.

"What is it?" demanded Georgie the curious. "Read it out loud."

"NEW HAVEN, November 29.

"Broke collar-bone playing foot-ball. Honest Injun. Terribly sorry. Better luck next time."

"RAOUL."

"There will not," observed Patty, "be a next time."

III The Impressionable Mr. Todhunter

HAS the mail been around yet?" called Priscilla to a girl at the other end of the corridor.

"Don't believe so. It has n't been in our room."

"There she comes now!" and Priscilla swooped down upon the mail-girl. "Got anything for 399?"

"Do you want Miss Wyatt's mail too?"

"Yes; I 'll take everything. What a lot! Is that all for us?" And Priscilla walked down the corridor swinging her note-book by its shoe-string, and opening envelops as she went. She was presently joined by Georgie Merriles, likewise swinging a note-book by a shoe-string.

"Hello, Pris; going to English? Want me to help carry your mail?"

"Thank you," said Priscilla; "you may keep the most of it. Now, that," she added, holding out a blue envelop, "is an advertisement for cold cream which no lady should be without; and that"–holding out a yellow envelop–"is an advertisement for beef extract which no brainworker should be without; and that"–holding out a white envelop–"is the worst of all, because it looks like a legitimate letter, and it 's nothing but a 'Dear Madam' thing, telling me my tailor has moved from Twenty-second to Forty-third Street, and hopes I 'll continue to favor him with my patronage.

"And here," she went on, turning to her room-mate's correspondence, "is a cold-cream and a beef-extract letter for Patty, and one from Yale; that's probably Raoul explaining why he could n't come to the Prom. It won't do any good, though. No mortal man can ever make her believe he did n't have his collar-bone broken on purpose. And I don't know whom that 's from," Priscilla continued, examining the last letter. "It 's marked 'Hotel A–, New York.' Never heard of it, did you? Never saw the writing before, either."

Georgie laughed. "Do you keep tab on all of Patty's correspondents?"

"Oh, I know the most of them by this time. She usually reads the interesting ones out loud, and the ones that are n't interesting she never answers, so they stop writing. Hurry up; the bell's going to ring"; and they pushed in among the crowd of girls on the steps of the recitation-hall.

The bell did ring just as they reached the class-room, and Priscilla dropped the letters, without comment, into Patty's lap as she went past. Patty was reading poetry and did not look up. She had assimilated some ten pages of Shelley since the first bell rang, and as she was not sure which would be taken up in class, she was now swallowing Wordsworth in the same voracious manner. Patty's method in Romantic Poetry was to be very fresh on the first part of the lesson, catch the instructor's eye early in the hour, make a brilliant recitation, and pass the remainder of the time in gentle meditation.

To-day, however, the unwonted bulk of her correspondence diverted her mind from its immediate duty. She failed to catch the instructor's eye, and the recitation proceeded without her assistance. Priscilla watched her from the back seat as she read the Yale letter with a skeptical frown, and made a grimace over the blue and the yellow; but before she had reached the Hotel A–, Priscilla was paying attention to the recitation again. It was coming her way, and she was anxiously forming an opinion on the essential characteristics of Wordsworth's view of immortality.

Suddenly the room was startled by an audible titter from Patty, who hastily composed her face and assumed a look of vacuous innocence–but too late. She had caught the instructor's eye at last.

"Miss Wyatt, what do you consider the most serious limitations of our author?"

Miss Wyatt blinked once or twice. This question out of its context was not illuminating. It was a part of her philosophy, however, never to flunk flat; she always crawled.

"Well," she began with an air of profound deliberation, "that question might be considered in two ways, either from an artistic or a philosophic standpoint."

This sounded promising, and the instructor smiled encouragingly. "Yes?" she said.

"And yet," continued Patty, after still profounder deliberation, "I think the same reason will be found to be the ultimate explanation of both."

The instructor might have inquired, "Both what?" but she refrained and merely waited.

Patty thought she had done enough, but she plunged on desperately: "In spite of his really deep philosophy we notice a certain—one might almost say dash about his poetry and a lack of—er—meditation which I should attribute to his immaturity and his a—rather wild life. If he had lived longer I think he might have overcome it in time."

The class looked dazed, and the corners of the instructor's mouth twitched. "It is certainly an interesting point of view, Miss Wyatt, and, as far as I know, entirely original."

As they were crowding out at the end of the recitation Priscilla pounced upon Patty. "What on earth were you saying about Wordsworth's youth and immaturity?" she demanded. "The man lived to be over eighty, and composed a poem with his last gasp."

"Wordsworth? I was talking about Shelley."

"Well, the class was n't."

"How should I know?" Patty demanded indignantly. "She said 'our author,' and I avoided specific details as long as I could."

"Oh, Patty, Patty! and you said he was wild—the lamblike Wordsworth!"

"What were you laughing at, anyway?" demanded Georgie.

Patty smiled again. "Why, this," she said, unfolding the Hotel A—letter. "It 's from an Englishman, Mr. Todhunter, some one my father discovered last summer and invited out to stay with us for a few days. I 'd forgotten all about him, and here he writes to know whether and when he may call, and, if so, will it be convenient for him to come to-night. That 's a comprehensive sentence, is n't it? His train gets in at half-past five and he 'll be out about six."

"He is n't going to take any chances," said Priscilla.

"No," said Patty; "but I don't mind. I invited him to come out to dinner some night, though I 'd forgotten it. He 's really very nice, and, in spite of what the funny papers say about Englishmen, quite entertaining."

"Intentionally or unintentionally?" inquired Georgie.

"Both," said Patty.

"What 's he doing in America?" asked Priscilla. "Not writing a book on the American Girl, I hope."

"Not quite as bad as that," said Patty. "He 's corresponding for a newspaper, though." She smiled dreamily. "He 's very curious about college."

"Patty, I hope you were not guilty of trying to make an Englishman, a guest in your father's house, believe any of your absurd fabrications!"

"Of course not," said Patty; "I was most careful in everything I told him. But," she acknowledged, "he–he gets impressions easily."

"It is easy to get impressions when one is talking with you," observed Georgie.

"He asked me," Patty continued, ignoring this remark, "what we studied in college! But I remembered that he was an alien in a foreign land, and I curbed my natural instincts, and outlined the courses in the catalogue verbatim, and I explained the different methods of instruction, and described the library and laboratories and lecture-rooms."

"Was he impressed?" asked Priscilla.

"Yes," said Patty; "I think you might almost say dazed. He asked me apologetically if we ever did anything to relieve the strain,–had any amusements, you know,–and I said, oh, yes; we had a

Browning and an Ibsen club, and we sometimes gave Greek tragedies in the original. He was positively afraid to come near me again, for fear I 'd forget and talk to him in Greek instead of English."

In view of the facts, Patty's friends considered this last remark distinctly humorous, for she had flunked her freshman Greek three times, and had been advised by the faculty to take it over sophomore year.

"I hope, since he 's a newspaper writer," said Priscilla, "that you 'll do something to lighten his impression, or he 'll never favor women's colleges in England."

"I had n't thought of that," said Patty; "perhaps I ought."

They had reached the steps of the dormitory. "Let 's not go in," said Georgie; "let's go down to Mrs. Muldoon's and get some chocolate cake."

"Thank you," said Priscilla; "I 'm in training."

"Soup, then."

"Can't eat between meals."

"You come, then, Patty."

"Sorry, but I 've got to take my white dress down to the laundry and have it pressed."

"Are you going to dress up for him to the extent of evening clothes?"

"Yes," said Patty; "I think I owe it to the American Girl."

"Well," sighed Georgie, "I 'm hungry, but I suppose I might as well go in and dress that doll for the College Settlement Association. The show 's to-night."

"Mine 's done," said Priscilla; "and Patty would n't take one. Did you see Bonnie Connaught sitting on the back seat in biology this morning, hemming her doll's petticoat straight through the lecture?"

"Really?" laughed Patty. "It 's a good thing Professor Hitchcock 's nearsighted."

The College Settlement Association, by way of parenthesis, was in the habit of distributing three hundred dolls among the students every year before Christmas, to be dressed and sent to the settlement in New York. The dolls were supposed to be so well dressed that the East Side mothers could use them as models for the clothing of their own children, though it must be confessed that the tendency among the girls was to strive for effect and not for detail. On the evening before the dolls were to be shipped a doll show was regularly held, at which two cents admittance was charged (stamps accepted) to pay the expressage.

IT was ten minutes past six, and Phillips Hall (such of it as was not late) was dining, when the maid arrived with Mr. Algernon Vivian Todhunter's card. Patty, radiant in a white evening gown, was trying, with much squirming, to fasten it in the middle of the back.

"Oh, Sadie," she called to the maid, "would you mind coming in here and buttoning my dress? I can't reach it from above or below."

"You look just beautiful, Miss Wyatt," said Sadie, admiringly.

Patty laughed. "Do you think I can uphold the honor of the nation?"

"To be sure, miss," said Sadie, politely.

Patty ran down the corridor to the door of the reception-room, and then swept slowly in with what she called an air of continental repose. The room was empty. She glanced about in some surprise, for she knew that the two reception-rooms on the other side of the hall were being used for the doll show. She tiptoed over and peered in through the half-open door. The room was filled with dolls in rows and tiers; every piece of furniture was covered with them; and in a far corner, at the end of a long vista of dolls, appeared Mr. Algernon Vivian Todhunter, gingerly sitting on the edge of a sofa, surrounded by flaxen-haired baby dolls, and awkwardly holding in his lap the three he had displaced.

Patty drew back behind the door, and spent fully three minutes in regaining her continental repose; then she entered the room and greeted Mr. Todhunter effusively. He carefully transferred the dolls to his left arm and stood up and shook hands.

"Let me take the little dears," said Patty, kindly; "I 'm afraid they 're in your way."

Mr. Todhunter murmured something about its being a pleasure and a privilege to hold them.

Patty plumped up their clothes and rearranged them on the sofa with motherly solicitude, while Mr. Todhunter watched her gravely, his national politeness and his reportorial instinct each struggling for the mastery. Finally he began tentatively: "I say, Miss Wyatt, do–er–the young ladies spend much time playing with dolls?"

"No," said Patty, candidly; "I don't think you could say they spend too much. I have never heard of but one girl actually neglecting her work for it. You must n't think that we have as many dolls as this here every night," she went on. "It is rather an unusual occurrence. Once a year the girls hold what they call a doll show to see who has dressed her doll the best."

"Ah, I see," said Mr. Todhunter; "a little friendly rivalry."

"Purely friendly," said Patty.

As they started for the dining-room Mr. Todhunter adjusted his monocle and took a parting look at the doll show.

"I 'm afraid you think us childish, Mr. Todhunter," said Patty.

"Not at all, Miss Wyatt," he assured her hastily. "I think it quite charming, you know, and so–er–unexpected. I had always been told that they played somewhat peculiar games at these women's colleges, but I never supposed they did anything so feminine as to play with dolls."

WHEN Patty returned to her room that night, she found Georgie and Priscilla surrounded by grammars and dictionaries, doing German prose. Her appearance was hailed with a cry of indignant protest.

"When I have a man," said Priscilla, "I divide him up among my friends."

"Especially when he 's a curiosity," added Georgie.

"And we dressed up in grand clothes, and stood in your way coming out of chapel," went on Priscilla, "and you never even looked at us."

"Englishmen are so bashful," apologized Patty; "I did n't want to frighten him."

Priscilla looked at her suspiciously. "Patty, I hope you did n't impose on the poor man's credulity."

"Certainly not!" said Patty, with dignity. "I explained everything he asked me, and was most careful not to exaggerate. But," she added with engaging frankness, "I cannot be responsible for any impressions he may have obtained. When an Englishman once gets an idea, you know, it 's almost impossible to change it."

Mr. Algernon Vivian Todhunter, gingerly sitting on the edge of a chair

IV A Question of Ethics

PATTY'S class-room methods were the result of a wide experience in the professorial type of mind. By her senior year she had reduced the matter of recitation to a system, and could foretell with unvarying precision the day she would be called on and the question she would be asked. Her tactics varied with the subject and the instructor, and were the result of a penetration and knowledge of human nature that might have accomplished something in a worthier cause.

In chemistry, for example, her instructor was a man who had outlived any early illusions in regard to the superior conscientiousness of girls over boys. He was not by nature a suspicious person, but a long experience in teaching had inculcated an inordinate wariness which was sometimes out of season. He allowed no napping in his classes, and those who did not pay attention suffered. Patty discovered his weakness early in the year, and planned her campaign accordingly. As long as she did not understand the experiment in hand, she would watch him with a face beaming with intelligence; but when she did understand, and wished to recite, she would let her eyes wander to the window with a dreamy, far-away smile, and, being asked a question, would come back to the realities of chemistry with a start, and, after a moment of ostentatious pondering, make a brilliant recitation. It must be confessed that her moments of abstraction were rare; she was far too often radiantly interested.

In French her tactics were exactly opposite. The instructor, with all the native politeness of his race, called on those only who caught his eye and appeared willing and anxious to recite. This made the matter comparatively simple, but still required considerable finesse. Patty dropped her pen, spilled the pages from her notebook, tied her shoe-string, and even sneezed opportunely in order not to catch his eye at inconvenient moments. The rest of the class, who were not artists, contented themselves with merely lowering their eyes as he looked along the line–a method which in Patty's scornful estimation said as plainly as words, "Please don't call on me; I don't know."

But with Professor Cairnsley, who taught philosophy, it was more difficult to form a working hypothesis. He had grown old in the service of the college, and after thirty years' experience of girl-nature he was still as unsuspiciously trustful as he had been in the beginning. Taking it for granted that his pupils were as interested in the contemplation of philosophic truths as he himself, the professor conducted his recitations without a suspicion of guile, and based his procedure entirely upon the inspiration of the moment. The key to his method had always remained a mystery, and several generations of classes had searched for it in vain. Some averred that he called on every seventh girl; others, that he drew lots. Patty triumphantly announced early in the course that she had discovered the secret at last–that on Monday he called on the red-haired girls; on Tuesday, those with yellow hair; on Wednesday and Thursday, those with brown; and on Friday, those with black. But this solution, like the others, was found to break down in actual practice; and Patty, for one, discovered that it required all her ingenuity, and even a good deal of studying, to maintain her reputation for brilliancy in Professor Cairnsley's classes. And she cared about maintaining it, for she liked the professor and was one of his favorite pupils. She had known his wife before she entered college, and she often called upon them in their home, and, in short, exemplified the ideal relations between faculty and students.

Owing to the pressure of many interests, Patty's researches into philosophy were not as deep as the intentions of the course, but she had a very good working knowledge, which, in its details, would have astonished Professor Cairnsley could he have got behind the scenes. Though her knowledge was not based strictly on the text-book, her reputation in the class was good, and, as Patty admitted with a sigh, "It 's a great strain on the imagination to keep up a reputation in philosophy."

It had been established, indeed, as far back as her sophomore year, when the psychology class was awed into silence by its first introduction to the abstractions of science, and Patty alone had dared to lift her voice. The professor, one morning, had been placidly lecturing along on the subject of sensation, and in the course of the lecture had remarked: "It is probable that the individual experiences all the primary sensations during the first few months of infancy, and that in after life there is no such thing as a new sensation."

"Professor Cairnsley," Patty piped up, "did you ever shoot the chutes?"

The ice was broken at last, and the class felt at home, even in the somewhat deep waters of philosophy; and Patty, however undeservedly, had gained the credit of having a deeper insight than most into matters psychical.

And so into her senior year, when she entered upon the study of ethics, she carried along an unearned and fragile reputation, built upon subterfuges and likely to crumble at the slightest touch. She had maintained it very creditably up to the Christmas vacation, and had argued upon the ultimate ground of moral obligation and the origin of conscience quite as intelligently as though she had previously read what the text-book had to say on the subject. But when they had commenced the study of specific theologies, based upon definite historical facts, Patty found her imagination of little use, and on several occasions it had been purely good luck that had saved her from exposure. Once the bell had rung at an opportune moment, and twice she had been able to avert a direct answer by leading the discussion into side issues. She realized, however, that fortune would not always favor her, and as the professor usually forgot to call the roll, she formed the nefarious practice of cutting class when she did not have her lesson.

For a week or so in particular, her pressure of work in other directions (not all of them scholastic) had prevented her from devoting her usual amount of energy to the task of maintaining her philosophy reputation, and she had, without conscience, cut ethics several days in succession, and had failed to comment upon the fact to the professor.

"What did he lecture about in ethics–those recitations I missed?" she inquired of Priscilla, one afternoon.

"Swedenborg."

"Swedenborg," repeated Patty, dreamily. "He got up a new religion, did n't he? Or was it a new system of gymnastics? I 've heard about him, but I don't seem to remember any details."

"You 'd better make him up; he 's important."

"I dare say; but I 've lived twenty-one years without knowing about him, and I can wait a month longer. I 'm saving up

Confucius and the Jesuits for examination-time, and I 'll add Swedenborg to the list."

"You 'd better not. Professor Cairnsley 's fond of him, and is likely to pop a special examination at any moment."

"Not Professor Cairnsley," laughed Patty. "He does n't want to waste the time. He 's going to lecture straight on for two weeks—nice man; I see it in his eye. What I admire in a professor is a good, steady, plodding disposition that does n't go in for sensational surprises."

"You 'll find yourself mistaken some day," warned Priscilla.

"No danger, my dear Cassandra. I know Professor Cairnsley, and Professor Cairnsley thinks he knows me; and we just get along together beautifully. I wish there were more like him," Patty added with a sigh.

Professor Cairnsley began a lecture the next morning which was evidently calculated to extend through the hour, and Patty cast a triumphant glance at Priscilla as she unscrewed the top of her fountain-pen and settled down to work. In the course of the lecture, however, he had occasion to refer to Swedenborg, and, pausing a moment, he casually asked a girl on the front seat for a résumé of Swedenborg's philosophy. She, unfortunately confusing him with Schopenhauer, glibly attributed to him doctrines which would have outraged his soul could he have heard them. It is written that the worm will turn, and the professor's bland smile deserted him as he passed the question to a second girl without much better result. The class in general had evidently been laboring under Patty's delusion that the time had not come in which to learn back notes. Amazed and indignant, he pursued the matter with a persistency and a rancor he seldom showed. He began going straight through the class, growing more and more sarcastic with each recitation.

As she saw him finish with the row in front and begin on her row, Patty knew that she was doomed. She racked her brain for some memory of Swedenborg. He was a name to her and nothing more. He might have been an ancient Greek or a modern American, for all she knew. As Professor Cairnsley came along the line he was gradually eliciting from the terrified class the superficial points

32

which were more or less common to all philosophers. Patty perceived that her imagination could not help her out, that for once the placid professor was on the war-path, and that Swedenborg, and nothing but Swedenborg, would serve. She cast an agonized glance up at Priscilla, and Priscilla grinned back with "I told you so" written on every feature.

Patty looked about desperately. The lecture-room was shaped like an amphitheater, with part of the seats on a level with the main floor, and the rest rising in tiers. Patty sat on the main floor, well toward the rear. She could barely see the professor's head, but he was coming irrevocably. She did not have to see very clearly to know that. The girl before her answered wildly; the professor frowned, and, looking down at his roll-book, slowly and deliberately made a zero.

When he raised his eyes again Patty's seat was empty. She was kneeling on the floor, with her head bowed behind the girl in front. The unconscious professor passed over her bent head and called on the girl on the other side, who coughed hysterically once or twice, and flunked flat; and while he was crediting the fact in his roll-book Patty resumed her seat. A ripple of laughter ran around the room; the professor frowned, and remarked that he saw no occasion for amusement. The bell rang, and the class somewhat sheepishly filed out.

That afternoon Patty burst into the study where Priscilla and Georgie Merriles were making tea. "Did you ever think I had much of a conscience?" she demanded.

"Never thought it was your strong point," said Georgie.

"Well, I 've got a perfectly tremendous one! What do you think I 've been doing?"

"Making up your ethics lectures," suggested Priscilla.

"Worse than that."

"You have n't been to gym, Patty!" said Georgie.

"Goodness, no! I 'm not so far gone as that. Well, I 'll tell you. I met Professor Cairnsley by the gate and walked in with him, and, if you please, he complimented me on my work in ethics!"

"That ought to have been embarrassing," said Georgie.

"It was," acknowledged Patty. "I told him I did n't really know as much as he thought I did."

"What did he say?"

"He said I was too modest. He 's such a trustful old man, you know, that you sort of hate to deceive him. And what do you think? I told him about the seat!"

Priscilla smiled approvingly upon her usually recreant room-mate. "Well, Patty, you certainly are better than I gave you credit for!"

"Thank you," murmured Patty.

"I begin to believe you have got a conscience," said Georgie.

"An excellent one," said Patty, complacently.

"It pays in the end," said Priscilla.

"It does," agreed Patty. "Professor Cairnsley said he would explain Swedenborg to me himself, and he invited me over to dinner to-night!"

V The Elusive Kate Ferris

THE mysterious Kate Ferris, who kept Priscilla on the verge of nervous prostration for a whole semester, entered upon her college career in an entirely unpremeditated and impromptu manner. It began one day away back in November. Georgie Merriles and Patty had just strolled home from the athletic field, where they had been witnessing the start of a paper-chase cross country, in which Priscilla was impersonating a fox. As they entered the study, Georgie stopped to examine some loose sheets of paper which were impaled upon the door.

"What 's this, Patty?"

"Oh, that 's the registration-list for the German Club. Priscilla 's secretary, you know, and every one who wants to join comes here. The study has been so full of freshmen all the time that I told her to hang it on the door and let them join outside; it works beautifully." Patty turned the leaves and ran her eyes down the list of sprawling signatures. "It 's a popular organization, is n't it? The freshmen are simply scrambling to get in."

"They 're trying to show Fräulein Scherin how much interest they take in the subject," Georgie laughed.

Patty picked up the pencil. "Would you like to join? I know Priscilla would be gratified."

"No, thank you; I pay club dues enough already."

"I 'm afraid I 'm not exactly eligible myself, as I don't know any German. It 's such a beautifully sharp pencil, though, that I hate not to write with it." Patty poised the pencil a moment, and abstractedly traced the name "Kate Ferris."

Georgie laughed, "If there should happen to be a Kate Ferris in college, she would be surprised to find herself a member of the German Club," and the incident was forgotten.

A few days later the two came in from class, to find Priscilla and the president of the German Club sitting on the divan with their heads together, frantically turning the leaves of the catalogue.

"She is n't a sophomore," the president announced. "She must be a freshman, Priscilla. Look again."

"I 've gone over this list three times, and there is n't a single Ferris down."

Georgie and Patty exchanged glances and inquired the trouble.

"A girl named Kate Ferris has registered for the German Club, and we 've gone through all the classes, and there simply is n't any such girl in college."

"Possibly a special," Patty suggested.

"Of course! Why did n't we think of that?" And Priscilla turned to the list of special students. "No; she is n't here."

"Let me look"; and Patty ran her eyes down the column. "You 've mistaken the name," she remarked, handing the book back with a shrug.

Priscilla produced the registration-list, and triumphantly exhibited an unmistakable Kate Ferris.

"They forgot to put her in the catalogue."

"I never knew them to make such a mistake before," said the president, dubiously. "I don't believe we 'd better put her in the roll-book till we find out who she is."

"Then you 'll hurt her feelings," said Georgie. "Freshmen are terribly sensitive about being slighted."

"Oh, very well; it does n't matter." And Kate Ferris was accordingly enrolled in the club records.

Several weeks later Priscilla was engaged in laboriously turning the minutes of the last meeting into grammatical German, and as she closed the dictionary and grammar with a sigh of relief, she remarked to Patty: "Do you know, it 's very queer about that Kate Ferris. She has n't paid her dues, and, as far as I can make out, she has n't attended a single meeting. Would n't you take her name off the roll? I don't believe she 's in college any more.

"You might as well," said Patty, and she listlessly watched Priscilla as she scratched out the name with a penknife. Patty never made the mistake of overacting.

The next morning, as Priscilla came in from a class, she found a note on her door-block, written in the perpendicular characters of Kate Ferris. It ran:

DEAR MISS POND: I came to pay my German Club dues, and as you are not in, I have left the money on the bookcase. Am sorry to have missed so many meetings, but have not been able to attend classes lately. KATE FERRIS. Priscilla exhibited the note to the president as a tangible proof that Kate Ferris still existed, and reinscribed the name in the roll-book.

A few weeks later she found a second note on her door-block:

DEAR MISS POND: As I am very busy with my class work, I find that I have not time to attend the German Club meetings, and so have decided to resign. I left my letter of resignation on the bookcase. KATE FERRIS.

As Priscilla scratched the name out of the roll-book again she remarked to Patty: "I am glad this Kate Ferris has left the club at last. She has caused me more trouble than all the rest of the members put together."

The next morning a third note appeared on the block:

DEAR MISS POND: I happened to mention the fact of my having resigned from the German Club to Fräulein Scherin last night, and she said that the club would help me in my work, and advised me to stay in it. So I shall be much obliged if you will not present my letter at the meeting after all, as I have decided to follow her advice. KATE FERRIS.

Priscilla tossed the note to Patty with a groan, and getting out the roll-book, she turned to the F's and reënrolled Kate Ferris.

Patty sympathetically watched the process over her shoulder. "The book is getting so thin in that spot," she laughed, "that Kate Ferris is actually coming through on the other side. If she changes her mind many more times there won't be anything left."

"I 'm going to ask Fräulein Scherin about her," Priscilla declared. "She 's made me so much trouble that I 'm curious to see what she looks like."

She did ask Fräulein Scherin, but Fräulein denied all knowledge of the girl. "I have so many freshmen," she apologized, "I cannot all of them with their queer names remember."

Priscilla inquired about Kate Ferris from the freshmen she knew, but though all of them thought that the name sounded familiar, none of them could exactly place her. She was variously described as tall and dark and small and light, but further inquiry always proved that the girl they had in mind was some one else.

Priscilla kept hearing about the girl on all sides, but could never catch a glimpse of her. Miss Ferris called several times on business, but Priscilla always happened to be out. Her name was posted on the bulletin-board for having library books that were overdue. She even wrote a paper for one of the German Club meetings (Georgie was not a facile German scholar, and it had required a whole Saturday); but owing to the fact that she was suddenly called out of town, she did not read it in person.

A month or two after Kate Ferris's advent, Priscilla had friends visiting her from New York, for whom she gave a tea in the study.

"I am going to invite Kate Ferris," she announced. "I insist upon finding out what she looks like."

"Do," said Patty. "I should like to find out myself."

The invitation was despatched, and on the next day Priscilla received a formal acceptance.

"It 's strange that she should send an acceptance for a tea," she remarked as she read it, "but I 'm glad to get it, anyway. I like to feel sure that I 'm to see her at last."

On the evening of the tea, after the guests had gone and the furniture had been moved back, the weary hostesses, in somewhat rumpled evening dresses (a considerable crush results when fifty are entertained in a room whose utmost capacity is fifteen), were reëntertaining one or two friends on the lettuce sandwiches and cakes the obliging guests had failed to consume. The company and the clothes having passed in review, the conversation flagged a little, and Georgie suddenly asked: "Was Kate Ferris here? I was so busy passing cakes that I did n't look, and I wanted to see her especially!"

"That 's so!" Patty exclaimed. "I did n't see her, either. She 's the most abnormally inconspicuous person I ever heard of. What did she look like, Pris?"

Priscilla knit her brows. "She could n't have come. I kept watching for her all the evening. It 's strange, is n't it?–when she was so careful to send an acceptance. I 'm growing positively morbid over the girl; I begin to think she 's invisible."

"I begin to think so myself," said Patty.

The next morning's mail brought a bunch of violets and an apology from Kate Ferris. "She had been unavoidably detained."

"It 's positively uncanny!" Priscilla declared. "I shall go to the registrar and tell her that this Kate Ferris is neither down in the catalogue nor the college directory, and find out where she lives."

"Don't do anything reckless," Georgie pleaded. "Take what the gods send and be grateful."

But Priscilla was as good as her word, and she returned from the registrar's office flushed and defiant. "She insists that there is n't any such person in college, and that I must have made a mistake in the name! Did you ever hear anything so absurd?"

"That seems to me the only reasonable explanation," Patty agreed amicably. "Perhaps it is Harris instead of Ferris."

Priscilla faced her ominously. "You read the name yourself. It was as plain as printing."

"We 're all liable to make mistakes," Patty murmured soothingly.

"Do you know," said Georgie, "I begin to think it 's all a hallucination, and that there really is n't any Kate Ferris. It 's strange, of course, but not any stranger than some of those cases you read about in psychology."

"Hallucinations don't send flowers," said Priscilla, hotly; and she stalked out of the room, leaving Patty and Georgie to review the campaign.

"I 'm afraid it 's gone far enough," said Georgie. "If she bothers the office very much there 'll be an official investigation."

"I 'm afraid so," sighed Patty. "It 's been very entertaining, but she is really getting sensitive on the subject, and I don't dare mention Kate Ferris's name when we 're alone."

"Shall we tell her?"

Patty shook her head. "Not just now–I should n't dare. She believes in corporal punishment."

A few days later Priscilla received another note directed in the hand she had come to dread. She threw it into the waste-basket unopened; but, curiosity prevailing, she drew it out again and read it:
DEAR MISS POND: As I have been obliged to leave college on account of my health, I inclose my resignation to the German Club. I thank you very sincerely for your kindness to me this year, and shall always look back upon our friendship as one of the happiest memories of my college life. Yours sincerely, KATE FERRIS.

When Patty came in she found Priscilla silently and grimly scratching a hole into the roll-book where Kate Ferris's name had been.
"Changed her mind again?" Patty asked pleasantly.

"She 's left college," Priscilla snapped, "and don't you ever mention her name to me again."

Patty sighed sympathetically and remarked to the room in general: "It 's sort of pathetic to have your whole college life summed up in a hole in the German Club archives. I can't help feeling sorry for her!"

VI A Story with Four Sequels

IT was Saturday, and Patty had been working ever since breakfast, with a brief pause for luncheon, on a paper entitled "Shakspere, the Man." At four o'clock she laid down her pen, pushed her manuscript into the waste-basket, and faced her room-mate defiantly.

"What do I care about Shakspere, the man? He 's been dead three hundred years."

Priscilla laughed unfeelingly. "What do I care about a frog's nervous system, for the matter of that? But I am writing an interesting monograph on it, just the same."

"Ah, I dare say you are making a valuable addition to the subject."

"It 's quite as valuable as your addition to Shaksperiana."

Patty dropped a voluble sigh and turned to the window to note that it was raining dismally.

"Oh, hand it in," said Priscilla comfortingly. "You 've worked on it all day, and it 's probably no worse than the most of your things."

"No sense to it," said Patty.

"They 're used to that," laughed Priscilla.

"What are you laughing at, anyway?" Patty asked crossly. "I don't see anything to laugh at in this beastly place. Always having to do what you don't want to do when you most don't want to do it. Just the same, day after day: get up by bells, eat by bells, sleep by bells. I feel like some sort of a delinquent living in an asylum."

Priscilla treated this outburst with the silence it deserved, and Patty turned back to her perusal of the rain-soaked campus.

"I wish something would happen," she said discontentedly. "I think I 'll put on a mackintosh and go out in search of adventure."

"Pneumonia will happen if you do."

"What business has it to be raining, anyway, when it ought to be snowing?"

As this was unanswerable, Priscilla returned to her frogs, and Patty drummed gloomily on the window-pane until a maid appeared with a card.

"A caller?" cried Patty "A missionary! A rescuer! A deliverer! Heaven send it 's for me!"

"Miss Pond," said Sadie, laying the card on the table.

Patty pounced upon. "'Mr. Frederick K. Stanthrope.' Who 's he, Pris?"

Priscilla wrinkled up her brows. "I don't know; I never heard of him. What do you suppose it can be?"

"An adventure–I know it 's an adventure. Probably your uncle, that you never heard of, has just died in the South Sea Islands, and left you a fortune because you 're his namesake; or else you 're a countess by rights, and were stolen from your cradle in infancy, and he 's the 1awyer come to tell you about it. I think it might have happened to me, when I 'm so bored to death! But hurry up and tell me about it, at least; a second-hand adventure 's better than no adventure at all. Yes, your hair is all right; never mind looking in the glass." And Patty pushed her room-mate out of the door, and, sitting down at her desk again, quite cheerfully pulled her discarded paper out of the waste-basket and began re-reading it with evident approval.

Priscilla returned before she had finished. "He did n't ask for me at all," she announced. "He asked for Miss McKay."

"Miss McKay?"

"That junior with the hair," she explained a trifle vaguely.

"How disgusting!" cried Patty. "I had it all planned how I was going to live with you in your castle up in the Hartz Mountains, and now it turns out that Miss McKay is the countess, and I don't even know her. What did the man look like, and what did he do?"

"Well, he looked rather frightened, and did n't do anything but stammer. There were two men in the reception-room, and of course I picked out the wrong one and begged his pardon and asked if he were Mr. Stanthrope. He said no; his name was Wiggins. So then the only thing left for me to do was to beg the other one's pardon.

"He was sitting in that high-backed green chair, with his eyes glued to his shoes, and holding his hat and cane in front of him like breastworks, as if he were preparing to repel an attack. He did n't look very approachable, but I boldly accosted him and asked if he were Mr. Stanthrope. He stood up and stammered and blushed and looked as if he wanted to deny it, but finally acknowledged that he was, and then stood politely waiting for me to state my business. I explained, and he stammered some more, and finally got out that he had called to see Miss McKay, and that the maid must have made a mistake. He was quite cross about it, you know, and acted as if I had insulted him; and the other man–the horrible Wiggins one–laughed, and then looked out of the window and pretended he had n't. I apologized,–though I could n't for the life of me see what there was to apologize for,–and told him I would send the maid for Miss McKay, and backed out."

"Is that all?" Patty asked disappointedly. "If I could n't have a better adventure than that, I should n't have any."

"But the funny thing is that when I told Sadie, she insisted that he had asked for me."

"Ha! The plot thickens, after all. What does it mean? Did he look like detective, or merely a pickpocket?"

"He looked like a very ordinarily embarrassed young man."

Patty shook her head dejectedly. "There 's a mystery somewhere, but I don't see that it affords much entertainment. I dare say that when Miss McKay came he told her he had n't asked for her at all; he had asked for Miss Higginbotham. The only explanation I can think of is that he is insane, and there are so many insane people in the world that it is n't even interesting."

Patty recounted the story of Priscilla's caller at the dinner-table that night.

"I know the sequel," said Lucille Carter. "The other man, the Mr. Wiggins, is Bonnie Connaught's cousin; and he told her about some young man who came out in the car with him, and asked for Miss Pond at the door, and then all of a sudden seemed to change his mind, and went tearing down the corridor after the maid, yelling, "Hi, there! Hi, there!" at the top of his voice; but he could n't catch her, and when Miss Pond came he pretended he had asked for some one else."

"Is that all?" asked Patty. "I don't think it is much of a sequel. It just proves that there 's a plot against Priscilla's life, and I already knew that. I intend to ask Miss McKay about him. I don't know her, except by sight, but in a case of life and death like this, I don't think it 's necessary to wait for an introduction."

The next evening Patty announced "Sequel number two! Mr. Frederick K. Stanthrope lives in New York, and is Miss McKay's brother's best friend. She has only met him once before, and does n't know any of his past affiliations. But the queer thing is that he never mentioned to her anything about Priscilla. Should n't you naturally think he would have told her about such a funny mistake?

"In my opinion," Patty continued solemnly, "it was plainly premeditated. He 's undoubtedly a villain in disguise, and he used his acquaintance with Miss McKay as a cloak to elude detection. My theory is this: He got Priscilla's name out of the catalogue, and came here intending to murder her for her jools; but when he saw how big she was he was scared and so abandoned his dastardly intent. Now if he had chosen me, my body would, at this moment, have been concealed behind the sofa, and my class pin reposing in the murderer's pocket."

Patty shuddered. "Think what I escaped. And all the time I was grumbling because nothing ever happens here!"

A few days later she appeared at the table with a further announcement: "I have the pleasure of offering for your perusal, young ladies, the third and last sequel in the great Stanthrope-Pond-McKay mystery. And I hereby take the opportunity of apologizing to Mr. Stanthrope for my unworthy suspicions. He is not a burglar, nor a detective, nor a murderer, nor even a lawyer, but just a poor young man with a buried romance."

"How did you find out?"–in a chorus of voices.

"I just met Miss McKay in the hall, and she has been in New York, where her brother told her the particulars. It seems that three or four years ago Mr. Frederick K. Stanthrope was engaged to a girl here in college named Alice Pond–she is now Mrs. Hiram Brown, but that has nothing to do with the story.

"Being in town last Saturday on business, he decided to run out and call on Miss McKay, as he was such a friend of her brother's– and also for the sake of old times. He amused himself all the way out in the car by resurrecting his buried romance, and he kept getting more and more pensive with every mile. When he finally reached the door and handed his card to the maid, he abstractedly called for Miss Pond just as he used to do four years ago. He did n't realize at first what he had done. Then it came over him in a flash, but he could n't catch Sadie. He knew, of course, that the other man had heard, and he sat there scared to death; trying to think of some plausible excuse, and momentarily expecting a strange Miss Pond to pop in and demand an explanation.

"Sure enough, the curtains parted, and a tall, beautiful, stately creature (I quote Miss McKay's brother) swept into the room, and, approaching the wrong man, asked him in haughty tones if he were Mr. Frederick K. Stanthrope. He very properly denied it, whereupon there was nothing for the right Mr. Stanthrope to do but stand up and acknowledge it like a man, which he did; but there he stuck. His imagination was numbed, paralyzed, so he turned it off on poor Sadie, and all the time he knew that the other man knew that he was lying. And that is all," Patty finished. "It 's not much of a story, but such as it is, it 's a blessing to have it concluded."

"Patty," called Priscilla, from the other end of the table, "have you been telling them that absurd story?"

"Why not?" asked Patty. "Having heard so many sequels, they naturally wanted to hear the last."

Priscilla laughed. "But yours does n't happen to be the last. I know a still later one."

"Later than Patty's?" the table demanded.

"Yes, later than Patty's. It is n't really a sequel; it 's just an appendix. I should n't tell you, only you 'll find it out, so I might as well. Miss McKay has invited two men for the junior party, and both have accepted. As two men are hard to manage, she has (by request) asked me to take care of one of them–namely, Mr. Frederick K. Stanthrope."

Patty sighed. "I see a whole series of sequels stretching away into the future. It 's worse than the Elsie Books!"

VII In Pursuit of Old English

HELLO, Patty! Have you read the bulletin-board this morning?" called Cathy Fair, as she caught up with Patty on the way home from a third-hour recitation.

"No," said Patty; "I think it 's a bad habit. You see too many unpleasant things there."

"Well, there 's certainly an unpleasant one to-day. Miss Skelling wishes the Old English class to be provided with writing materials this afternoon."

Patty stopped with a groan. "I think it 's absolutely abominable to give an examination without a word of warning."

"Not an examination," quoted Cathy; "just a 'little test to see how much you know.'"

"I don't know a thing," wailed Patty–"not a blessed thing."

"Nonsense, Patty; you know more than any one else in the class."

"Bluff–it 's all pure bluff. I come in strong on the literary criticism and the general discussions, and she never realizes that I don't know a word of the grammar."

"You 've got two hours. You can cut your classes and review it up."

"Two hours!" said Patty, sadly. "I need two days. I 've never learned it, I tell you. The Anglo-Saxon grammar is a thing no mortal can carry in his head, and I thought I might as well wait and learn it before examinations."

"I don't wish to appear unfeeling," laughed Cathy, "but I should say, my dear, that it serves you right."

"Oh, I dare say," said Patty. "You are as bad as Priscilla"; and she trailed gloomily homeward.

She found her friends reviewing biology and eating olives. "Have one?" asked Lucille Carter, who, provided with a hatpin by way of fork, was presiding over the bottle for the moment.

"No, thanks," returned Patty, in the tone of one who has exhausted life and longs for death.

"What 's the matter?" inquired Priscilla. "You don't mean to say that woman has given you another special topic?"

"Worse than that!" and Patty laid bare the tragedy.

A sympathetic silence followed; they realized that while she was, perhaps, not strictly deserving of sympathy, still her impending fate was of the kind that might overtake any one.

"You know, Pris," said Patty, miserably, "that I simply can't pass."

"No," said Priscilla, soothingly ; "I don't believe you can."

"I shall flunk flat–absolutely flat. Miss Skelling will never have any confidence in me again, and will make me recite every bit of grammar for the rest of the semester."

"I should think you 'd cut," ventured Georgie–that being, in her opinion, the most obvious method of escaping an examination.

"I can't. I just met Miss Skelling in the hall five minutes before the blow fell, and she knows I 'm alive and able to be about; besides, the class meets again to-morrow morning, and I 'd have to cram all night or cut that too."

"Why don't you go to Miss Skelling and frankly explain the situation," suggested Lucille the virtuous, "and ask her to let you off for a day or two? She would like you all the better for it."

"Will you listen to the guileless babe!" said Patty. "What is there to explain, may I ask? I can't very well tell her that I prefer not to learn the lessons as she gives them out, but think it easier to wait and cram them up at one fell swoop, just before examinations. That would ingratiate myself in her favor!"

"It 's your own fault," said Priscilla.

Patty groaned. "I was just waiting to hear you say that! You always do."

"It 's always true. Where are you going?" as Patty started for the door.

"I am going," said Patty, "to ask Mrs. Richards to give me a new room-mate: one who will understand and appreciate me, and sympathize with my afflictions."

Patty walked gloomily down the corridor, lost in meditation. Her way led past the door of the doctor's office, which was standing invitingly open. Three or four girls were sitting around the room, laughing and talking and waiting their turns. Patty glanced in, and a radiant smile suddenly lightened her face, but it was instantly replaced by a look of settled sadness. She walked in and dropped into an arm-chair with a sigh.

"What 's the matter, Patty? You look as if you had melancholia."

Patty smiled apathetically. "Not quite so bad as that," she murmured, and leaned back and closed her eyes.

"Next," said the doctor from the doorway; but as she caught sight of Patty she walked over and shook her arm. "Is this Patty Wyatt? What is the matter with you, child?"

Patty opened her eyes with a start. "Nothing," she said; "I 'm just a little tired."

"Come in here with me."

"It 's not my turn," objected Patty.

"That makes no difference," returned the doctor.

Patty dropped limply into the consulting-chair.

"Let me see your tongue. Um-m–is n't coated very much. Your pulse seems regular, though possibly a trifle feverish. Have you been working hard?"

"I don't think I 've been working any harder than usual," said Patty, truthfully.

"Sitting up late nights?"

Patty considered. "I was up rather late twice last week," she confessed.

"If you girls persist in studying until all hours of the night, I don't know what we doctors can do."

Patty did not think it necessary to explain that it was a Welsh-rabbit party on each occasion, so she merely sighed and looked out of the window.

"Is your appetite good?"

"Yes," said Patty, in a tone which belied the words; "it seems to be very good."

"Um-m," said the doctor.

"I 'm just a little tired," pursued Patty, "but I think I shall be all right as soon as I get a chance to rest. Perhaps I need a tonic," she suggested.

"You 'd better stay out of classes for a day or two and get thoroughly rested."

"Oh, no," said Patty, in evident perturbation. "Our room is so full of girls all the time that it 's really more restful to go to classes; and, besides, I can't stay out just now."

"Why not?" demanded the doctor, suspiciously.

"Well," said Patty, a trifle reluctantly, "I have a good deal to do. I 've got to cram for an examination, and–"

The word "cram" was to the doctor as a red rag to a bull. "Nonsense!" she ejaculated. "I know what I shall do with you. You are going right over to the infirmary for a few days–"

"Oh, doctor!" Patty pleaded, with tears in her eyes, "there 's truly nothing the matter with me, and I 've got to take that examination."

"What examination is it?"

"Old English–Miss Skelling."

"I will see Miss Skelling myself," said the doctor, "and explain that you cannot take the examination until you come out. And now," she added, making a note of Patty's case, "I will have you put in the convalescent ward, and we will try the rest cure for a few days, and feed you up on chicken-broth and egg-nog, and see if we can get that appetite back."

"Thank you," said Patty, with the resigned air of one who has given up struggling against the inevitable.

What 's the matter, Patty?

"I like to see you take an interest in your work," added the doctor, kindly; "but you must always remember, my dear, that health is the first consideration."

Patty returned to the study and executed an impromptu dance in the middle of the floor.

"What 's the matter?" exclaimed Priscilla. "Are you crazy?"

"No," said Patty; "only ill." And she went into her bedroom and began slinging things into a dress-suit case.

Priscilla stood in the doorway and watched her in amazement. "Are you going to New York?" she asked.

"No," said Patty; "to the infirmary."

"Patty Wyatt, you 're a wretched little hypocrite!"

"Not at all," said Patty, cheerfully. "I did n't ask to go, but the doctor simply insisted. I told her I had an examination, but she said it did n't make any difference; health must be the first consideration."

"What 's in that bottle?" demanded Priscilla.

"That 's for my appetite," said Patty, with a grin; "the doctor hopes to improve it. I did n't like to discourage her, but I don't much believe she can." She dropped an Old English grammar and a copy of "Beowulf" into her suit-case.

"They won't let you study," said Priscilla.

"I shall not ask them," said Patty. "Good-by. Tell the girls to drop in occasionally and see me in my incarceration. Visiting hour from five to six." She stuck her head in again. "If any one wants to send violets, I think they might cheer me up."

THE next afternoon Georgie and Priscilla presented themselves at the infirmary, and were met at the door by the austere figure of the head nurse. "I will see if Miss Wyatt is awake," she said dubiously, "but I am afraid you will excite her; she 's to be kept very quiet."

"Oh, no; we 'll do her good," remonstrated Georgie; and the two girls tiptoed in after the nurse.

The convalescent ward was a large, airy room, furnished in green and white, with four or five beds, each surrounded with brass poles and curtains. Patty was lying in one of the corner beds near a window, propped up on pillows, with her hair tumbled about her face, and a table beside her covered with flowers and glasses of medicine. This elaborate paraphernalia of sickness created a momentary illusion in the minds of the visitors. Priscilla ran to the bedside and dropped on her knees beside her invalid room-mate.

"Patty dear," she said anxiously, "how do you feel?"

A seraphic smile spread over Patty's face. "I 've been able to take a little nourishment to-day," she said.

"Patty, you 're a scandalous humbug! Who gave you those violets? 'With love, from Lady Clara Vere de Vere'– that blessed freshman– and you 've borrowed every drop of alcohol the poor child ever thought of owning. And whom are those roses from? Miss Skelling! Patty, you ought to be ashamed."

Patty had the grace to blush slightly. "I was a trifle embarrassed," she admitted; "but when I reflected upon how sorry she would have been to find out how little I knew, and how glad she will be to find out how much I know, my conscience was appeased."

"Have you been studying?" asked Georgie.

"Studying!" Patty lifted up the corner of her pillow and exhibited a blue book. "Two days more of this, and I shall be the chief authority in America on Anglo-Saxon roots."

"How do you manage it?"

"Oh," said Patty, "when the rest-hour begins I lie down and shut my eyes, and they tiptoe over and look at me, and whisper, 'She 's asleep,' and softly draw the curtains around the bed; and I get out the book and put in two solid hours of irregular verbs, and am still sleeping when they come to look at me. They 're perfectly astonished at the amount I sleep. I heard the nurse telling the doctor that she did n't believe I 'd had any sleep for a month. And the worst of it is," she added, "that I am tired, whether you believe it or not, and I should just love to stay over here and sleep all day if I were n't so beastly conscientious about that old grammar."

"Poor Patty!" laughed Georgie. "She will be imposing on herself next, as well as on the whole college."

Friday morning Patty returned to the world.

"How's Old English?" inquired Priscilla.

"Very well, thank you. It was something of a cram, but I think I know that grammar by heart, from the preface to the index."

"You 're back in all your other work. Do you think it paid?"

"That remains to be seen," laughed Patty.

She knocked on Miss Skelling's door, and, after the first polite greetings, stated her errand: "I should like, if it is convenient for you, to take the examination I missed."

"Do you feel able to take it to-day?"

"I feel much better able to take it to-day than I did on Tuesday."

Miss Skelling smiled kindly. "You have done very good work in Old English this semester, Miss Wyatt, and I should not ask you to take the examination at all if I thought it would be fair to the rest of the class."

"Fair to the rest of the class?" Patty looked a trifle blank; she had not considered this aspect of the question, and a slow red flush crept over her face. She hesitated a moment, and rose uncertainly. "When it comes to that, Miss Skelling," she confessed, "I 'm afraid it would n't be quite fair to the rest of the class for me to take it."

Miss Skelling did not understand. "But, Miss Wyatt," she expostulated in a puzzled tone, "it was not difficult. I am sure you could pass."

Patty smiled. "I am sure I could, Miss Skelling. I don't believe you could ask me a question that I could n't answer. But the point is that it 's all learned since Tuesday. The doctor was laboring under a little delusion–very natural under the circumstances–when she sent me to the infirmary, and I spent my time there studying."

"But, Miss Wyatt, this is very unusual. I shall not know how to mark you," Miss Skelling murmured in some distress.

"Oh, mark me zero," said Patty, cheerfully. "It does n't matter in the least–I know such a lot that I 'll get through on the finals. Good-by; I 'm sorry to have troubled you." And she closed the door and turned thoughtfully homeward.

"Did it pay?" asked Priscilla.

Patty laughed and murmured softly:

"'The King of France rode up the hill with full ten thousand men; The King of France did gain the top, and then rode down again.'"

"What are you talking about?" demanded Priscilla.

"Old English," said Patty, as she sat down at her desk and commenced on the three days' work she had missed.

VIII The Deceased Robert

IT was ten o'clock, and Patty, having just read her ethics over for the third time without comprehending it, had announced sleepily, "I shall have to be good by inspiration; I can't seem to grasp the rule," when a knock sounded on the door and a maid appeared with the announcement, "Mrs. Richards wishes to see Miss Wyatt."

"At this hour!" Patty cried in dismay. "It must be something serious. Think, Priscilla. What have I been doing lately that would outrage the warden sufficiently to call me up at ten o'clock? You don't suppose I 'm going to be suspended or rusticated or expelled or anything like that, do you? I honestly can't think of a thing I 've done."

"It 's a telegram," the maid said sympathetically.

"A telegram?" Patty's face turned pale, and she left the room without a word.

Priscilla and Georgie sat on the couch and looked at each other with troubled faces. All ordinary telegrams came directly to the students. They knew that something serious must have happened to have it sent to the warden. Georgie got up and walked around the room uncertainly.

"Shall I go away, Pris?" she asked. "I suppose Patty would rather be alone if anything has happened. But if she 's going home and has to pack her trunk to-night, come and tell me and I will come down and help."

They stood at the door a few moments talking in low tones, and as Georgie started to turn away, Patty's step suddenly sounded in the corridor. She came in with a queer smile on her lips, and sat down on the couch.

"The warden has certainly reduced the matter of scaring people to a fine art," she said. "I was never more frightened in my life. I thought that the least that had happened was an earthquake which had engulfed the entire family."

"What was the matter?" Georgie and Priscilla asked in a breath.

Patty spread out a crumpled telegram on her knee, and the girls read it over her shoulder:

Robert died of an overdose of chloroform at ten this morning. Funeral to-morrow.

THOMAS M. WYATT.

"Thomas M. Wyatt," said Patty, grimly, "is my small brother Tommy, and Robert is short for Bobby Shafto, which was the name of Tommy's bull pup, the homeliest and worst-tempered dog that was ever received into the bosom of a respectable family."

"But why in the world did he telegraph?"

"It 's a joke," said Patty, shaking her head dejectedly. "Joking runs in the family, and we 've all inherited the tendency. One time my father–but, as my friend Kipling says, that 's another story. This dog, you see–this Robert Shafto–has cast a shadow over my vacations for more than a year. He killed my kitten, and ate my Venetian lace collar–it did n't even give him indigestion. He went out and wallowed in the rain and mud and came in and slept on my bed. He stole the beefsteak for breakfast and the rubbers and door-mats for blocks around. Property on the street appreciably declined, for prospective purchasers refused to purchase so long as Tommy Wyatt kept a dog. Robert was threatened with death time and again, but Tommy always managed to conceal him from impending justice until the trouble had blown over. But this time I suppose he committed some supreme enormity–probably chewed up the baby or one of my father's Persian rugs, or something like that. And Tommy, knowing how I detested the beast, evidently thought it would be a good joke to telegraph, though wherein lies the point I can't make out."

"Ah, I see," said Georgie; "and Mrs. Richards thought that Robert was a relation. What did she say?"

"She said, 'Come in, Patty dear,' when I knocked on the door. Usually when I have had the honor of being received by her she has somewhat frigidly called me 'Miss Wyatt.' I opened the door with my knees shaking when I heard that 'Patty dear,' and she took my hand and said. 'I am sorry to have to tell you that I have heard bad news from your brother.'

"'Tommy?' I gasped.

"'No; Robert.'

"I was dazed. I racked my brains, but I could n't remember any brother Robert.

"'He is very ill,' she went on. 'Yes, I must tell you the truth, Patty; poor little Robert passed away this morning'; and she laid the telegram before me. Then, when it flashed over me what it meant, I was so relieved that I put my head down on her desk and simply laughed till I cried; and she thought I was crying all the time, and kept patting my head and quoting Psalms. Well, then I did n't dare to tell her, after she had expended all that sympathy; so as soon as I could stop laughing (which was n't very soon, for I had got considerable momentum) I raised my head and told her–trying to be truthful and at the same time not hurt her feelings–that Robert was not a brother, but just a sort of friend. And, do you know, she immediately jumped to the conclusion that he was a fiancé, and began stroking my hair and murmuring that it was sometimes harder to lose friends than relatives, but that I was still young, and I must not let it blast my life, and that maybe in the future when time had dulled the pain–and then, remembering that it would n't do to advise me to adopt a second fiancé before I had buried my first, she stopped suddenly and asked if I wished to go home to the funeral.

"I told her no, that I did n't think it would be best; and she said perhaps not if it had n't been announced, and she kissed me and told me she was glad to see me bearing up so bravely."

"Patty!" Priscilla exclaimed in horror, "it 's dreadful. How could you let her think it?"

"How could I help it?" Patty demanded indignantly. "What with being frightened into hysterics first, and then having a strange fiancé thrust at me without a moment's notice, I think that I carried off the situation with rare delicacy and finesse. Do you think it would have been tactful to tell her it was nothing but a bull pup she was quoting Scripture about?"

"I don't see how it was exactly your fault," Georgie acknowledged.

"Thank you," said Patty. "If you had a brother like Tommy Wyatt you would know how to sympathize with me. I suppose I ought to be grateful to know that the dog is dead, but I should like to have had the news broken a little less gently."

"Patty," exclaimed Priscilla, as a sudden thought struck her, "do you happen to remember that you are on the reception committee of the Dramatic Club cotillion to-morrow night? What will Mrs. Richards think when she sees you in evening dress, receiving at a party, on the very day your fiancé has been buried?"

"I wonder?" said Patty, doubtfully. "Do you really think I ought to stay away? After working like a little buzz-saw making tissue-paper favors for the thing, I hate to have to miss it just because my brother's bull pup, that I never even liked, is dead.

"I 'll go," she added, brightening, "and receive the guests with a forced and mechanical smile; and every time I feel the warden's eyes upon me I shall with difficulty choke back the tears, and she will say to herself:

"'Brave girl! How nobly she is struggling to present a composed face to the world! None would dream, to look at that seemingly radiant creature, that, while she is outwardly so gay, she is in reality concealing a great sorrow which is gnawing at her very vitals.'"

IX Patty the Comforter

IT was on the eve of the mid-year examinations, and a gloom had fallen over the college. The conscientious ones who had worked all the year were working harder than ever, and the frivolous ones who had played all the year were working with a desperate frenzy calculated to render their minds a blank when the crucial hour should have arrived. But Patty was not working. It was a canon of her college philosophy, gained by three and a half years' of personal experience, that the day before examinations is not the time to begin to study. One has impressed the instructor with one's intelligent interest in the subject, or one has not, and the result is as sure as if the marks were already down in black and white in the college archives. And so Patty, who at least lived up to her lights, was, with the exception of a few points which she intended to learn for this period only, conscientiously neglecting the "judicious review" recommended by the faculty.

Her friends, however, who, though perhaps equally philosophic, were less consistent, were subjecting themselves to what was known as a "regular freshman cram"; and as no one had any time to talk to Patty, or to make anything to eat, she found it an unprofitable period. Her own room-mate even drove her from the study because she laughed out loud over the book she was reading; and, an exile, she wandered around to the studies of her friends, and was confronted by an "engaged" on every door. She was sitting on a window-sill in the corridor, pondering on the general barrenness of things, when she suddenly remembered her friends the freshmen in study 321. She had not visited them for some time, and freshmen are usually interesting at this period. She accordingly turned down the corridor that led to 321, and found a "POSITIVELY ENGAGED TO EVERY ONE!!" in letters three inches high, across the door. This promised a richness of entertainment within, and Patty heaved a disappointed sigh loud enough to carry through the transom.

The turning of leaves and rustling of paper ceased; evidently they were listening, but they gave no sign. Patty wrote a note on the door-block with reverberating punctuation-points, and then retired noisily, and tiptoed back a moment later, and leaned against the wall. Curiosity prevailed; the door opened, and a face wearing a hunted look peered out.

"Oh, Patty Wyatt, was that you?" she asked. "We thought it was Frances Stoddard coming down to have geometry explained, and so we kept still. Come in."

"Goodness, no; I would n't come in over an 'engaged' like that for anything. I 'm afraid you 're busy."

The freshman grasped her by the arm. "Patty, if you love us come in and cheer us up. We 're so scared we don't know what to do."

Patty consented to be drawn across the threshold. "I don't want to interrupt you," she remonstrated, "if you have anything to do." The study was occupied by three girls. Patty smiled benignly at the two haggard faces before her. "Where 's Lady Clara Vere de Vere?" she asked. "She surely is n't wasting these precious last moments in anything frivolous."

"She 's in her bedroom, with a geometry in one hand and a Greek grammar in the other, trying to learn them both at once."

"Tell her to come out here; I want to give her some good advice"; and Patty sat down on the divan and surveyed the dictionary-bestrewn room with an appreciative smile.

"Oh, Patty, I 'm so glad to see you!" Lady Clara exclaimed, appearing in the doorway. "The sophomores have been telling us the most dreadful stories about examinations. They are n't true, are they?"

"Mercy, no! Don't believe a word those sophomores tell you. They were freshmen themselves last year, and if the examinations were as bad as they say, they would n't have passed them, either."

A relieved expression stole over the three faces.

"You 're such a comfort, Patty. Upper-classmen take things easily, don't they?"

"One gets inured to almost anything in time," said Patty. "Examinations are even entertaining, if you know the right answers."

"But we won't know the right answers!" one of the freshmen wailed, her terror returning. "We simply don't know anything, and Latin comes to-morrow, and geometry the next day."

"Oh, well, in that case you can't get through anyway, so don't worry. You must take it philosophically, you know." Patty settled herself among the cushions and smiled upon her frightened auditors with easy nonchalance. "As an example of the uselessness of studying at the eleventh hour when you have n't done anything through the term, I will tell you my experience with freshman Greek. I was badly prepared when I came, I did n't study through the term, and, without exaggeration, I did n't know anything. Three days before examinations I suddenly comprehended the situation, and I began swallowing that grammar in chunks. I drank black coffee to keep awake, and worked till two in the morning, and scarcely stopped cramming irregular verbs for meals. I simply thought in Greek and dreamed in Greek. And, if you will believe it, after all that work I flunked in Greek! It shook my faith in studying for examinations. I 've never done it since, and I 've never flunked since. I believe that it 's just a matter of fate whether you get through or not, so I never bother any more."

The freshmen looked at one another disconsolately. "If it 's all decided beforehand, we 're lost."

Patty smiled reassuringly.

"A little flunking now and then Will happen to the best of men."

"But I 've heard they send people home, drop them, you know, if they flunk more than a certain amount. Is that so?" Lady Clara inquired in hushed tones.

"Oh, yes," said Patty; "they have to. I 've known some of the brightest girls in college to be dropped."

Lady Clara groaned. "I 'm awfully shaky in geometry, Patty. Do they flunk many girls in that?"

"Many!" said Patty. "The mere clerical labor of writing out the notes occupies the department two days."

"Is the examination terribly hard?"

"I don't remember much about it. It 's been such a long time since I was a freshman, you see. They picked out the hardest theorems, I know–things you could n't even draw, let alone demonstrate: the pyramid that 's cut in slices, for one,–I don't remember its name,– and that sprawling one that looks like a snail crawling out of its shell: the devil's coffin, I believe it 's called technically. And–oh, yes! they give you originals–frightful originals, like nothing you 've ever had before; and they put a little note at the top of the page telling you to do them first, and you get so muddled trying to think fast that you can't think at all. I know a girl who spent all the two hours trying to think out an original, and just as she got ready to write it down the bell rang and she had to hand in her paper."

"And what happened?"

"Oh, she flunked. You could n't really blame the instructor, you know, for not reading between the lines, for there were n't any lines to read between; but it was sort of a pity, for the girl really knew an awful lot–but she could n't express it."

"That 's just like me."

"Ah, it 's like a good many people." A silence ensued, and the freshmen looked at one another dejectedly. "But you can live, even if you should flunk math," Patty continued reassuringly. "Other people have done it before you."

"If it were only geometry–but we 're scared over Latin."

"Oh, Latin! There's no use studying for that, for you can't possibly read it all over, and if you just pick out a part, it 's sure not to be the same part they pick out. The best way is to say incantations over the book, and open it with your eyes blindfolded, and study the page it opens to; then, in case you don't pass,–and you probably won't–you can throw the blame on fate. My freshman year, if I remember right, they gave us for prose composition one of Emerson's essays to translate into Latin, and we could n't even tell what it meant in English."

The three looked at one another again.

"I could n't do anything like that."

"Nor I."

"Nor I."

"Nor any one else," said Patty.

"We can flunk Latin and math; but if we flunk any more we 're gone."

"I believe so," said Patty.

"And I 'm awfully shaky in German."

"And I in French."

"And I in Greek."

"I don't know anything about German," said Patty. "Never had it myself. But I remember hearing Priscilla say that the printed examination papers did n't come but in time, and Fräulein Scherin, who writes a frightful hand, wrote the questions on the board in German script, and they could n't even read them. In French I believe the first question was to write out the 'Marseillaise'; there are seven verses, and no one had learned them, and the 'Marseillaise,' you know, is a thing that you simply can't make up on the spur of the moment. As for Greek, I told you my own experience; I am sure nothing could be worse than that."

The freshmen looked at one another hopelessly. "There 's only English and hygiene and Bible history left."

"English is something you can't tell anything about," said Patty. "They 're as likely as not to ask you to write a heroic poem in iambic pentameters, if you know what they are. You have to depend on inspiration; you can't study for it."

"I hope," sighed Lady Clara, "to get through hygiene and Bible history, though, as they only count one hour apiece, I suppose it is n't much."

"You must n't be too sanguine," said Patty. "It all depends on chance. The class in hygiene is so big that the professor has n't time to read the papers; he just goes down the list and flunks every thirteenth girl. I 'm not sure about Bible history, but I think he does the same, because I know, freshman year, that I made a mistake and handed in my map of the Holy Lands done in colored chalk to the hygiene professor, and my chart of the digestive system to the Bible professor, and neither of them noticed it. They did look a good deal alike, but not so much but what you could tell them apart. All I have to say is that I hope none of you will be number thirteen."

The freshmen stared at one another in speechless horror, and Patty rose. "Well, good-by, my children, and, above all things, don't worry. I 'm glad if I 've been able to cheer you up a little, for so much depends on not being nervous. Don't believe any of the silly stories the sophomores tell," she called back over her shoulder; "they 're just trying to frighten you."

X "Per L'Italia"

COLLEGE is a more or less selfish place. Everybody is so busy with her own affairs that she has no time to give to her neighbor, unless her neighbor has something to give in return. Olivia Copeland apparently had nothing to give in return. She was quiet and inconspicuous, and it took a second glance to realize that her face was striking and that there was a look in her eyes that other freshmen did not have. By an unfelicitous chance she was placed in the same study with Lady Clara Vere de Vere and Emily Washburn. They thought her foreign and queer, and she thought them crude and boisterous, and after the first week or two of politely trying to get acquainted the effort was dropped on both sides.

The year wore on, and nobody knew, or at least no one paid any attention to the fact, that Olivia Copeland was homesick and unhappy. Her room-mates thought that they had done their duty when they occasionally asked her to play golf or go skating with them (an invitation they were very safe in giving, as she knew how to do neither). Her instructors thought that they had done their duty when they called her up to the desk after class and warned her that her work was not as good as it had been, and that if she wished to pass she must improve in it.

The English class was the only one in which she was not warned; but she had no means of knowing that her themes were handed about among the different instructors and that she was referred to in the department as "that remarkable Miss Copeland." The department had a theory that if they let a girl know she was doing good work she would immediately stop and rest upon her reputation; and Olivia, in consequence, did not discover that she was remarkable. She merely discovered that she was miserable and out of place, and she continued to drip tears of homesickness before a sketch of an Italian villa that hung above her desk.

It was Patty Wyatt who first discovered her. Patty had dropped into the freshmen's room one afternoon on some errand or other (probably to borrow alcohol), and had idly picked up a pile of English themes that were lying on the study table.

"Whose are these? Do you care if I look at them?" she asked.

"No; you can read them if you want to," said Lady Clara. "They 're Olivia's, but she won't mind."

Patty carelessly turned the pages, and then, as a title caught her eye, she suddenly looked up with a show of interest.

"'The Coral-fishers of Capri'! What on earth does Olivia Copeland know about the coral-fishers of Capri?"

"Oh, she lives somewhere near there—at Sorrento," said Lady Clara, indifferently.

"Olivia Copeland lives at Sorrento!" Patty stared. "Why did n't you tell me?"

"I supposed you knew it. Her father 's an artist or something of the sort. She 's lived in Italy all her life; that 's what makes her so queer."

Patty had once spent a sunshiny week in Sorrento herself, and the very memory of it was intoxicating. "Where is she?" she asked excitedly. "I want to talk to her."

"I don't know where she is. Out walking, probably. She goes off walking all by herself, and never speaks to any one, and then when we ask her to do something rational, like golf or basket-ball, she pokes in the house and reads Dante in Italian. Imagine!"

"Why, she must be interesting!" said Patty, in surprise, and she turned back to the themes.

"I think these are splendid!" she exclaimed.

"Sort of queer, I think," said Lady Clara. "But there 's one that 's rather funny. It was read in class—about a peasant that lost his donkey. I 'll find it"; and she rummaged through the pile.

Patty read it soberly, and Lady Clara watched her with a shade of disappointment.

"Don't you think it 's pretty good?" she asked.

"Yes; I think it 's one of the best things I ever read."

"You never even smiled!"

"My dear child, it is n't funny."

"Is n't funny! Why, the class simply roared over it."

Patty shrugged. "Your appreciation must have gratified Olivia. And here it 's February, and I 've barely spoken to her."

The next afternoon Patty was strolling home from a recitation, when she spied Olivia Copeland across the campus, headed for Pine Bluff and evidently out for a solitary walk.

"Olivia Copeland, wait a moment," Patty called. "Are you going for a walk? May I come too?" she asked, as she panted up behind.

Olivia assented with evident surprise, and Patty fell into step beside her. "I just found out yesterday that you live in Sorrento, and I wanted to talk to you. I was there myself once, and I think it 's the most glorious spot on earth."

Olivia's eyes shone. "Really?" she gasped. "Oh, I 'm so glad!" And before she knew it she was telling Patty the story of how she had come to college to please her father, and how she loved Italy and hated America; and what she did not tell about her loneliness and homesickness Patty divined.

She realized that the girl was remarkable, and she determined in the future to take an interest in her and make her like college. But a senior's life is busy and taken up with its own affairs, and for the next week or two Patty saw little of the freshman beyond an occasional chat in the corridors.

One evening she and Priscilla had returned late from a dinner in town, to be confronted by a dark room and an empty match-safe.

"Wait a moment and I 'll get some matches," said Patty; and she knocked on a door across the corridor where a freshman lived with whom they had a borrowing acquaintance. She found within her own freshman friends, Lady Clara Vere de Vere and Emily Washburn. It was evident by the three heads close together, and the hush that fell on the group as she entered, that some momentous piece of gossip had been interrupted. Patty forgot her room-mate waiting in the dark, and dropped into a chair with the evident purpose of staying out the evening.

"Tell me all about it, children," she said cordially.

The freshmen looked at one another and hesitated.

"A new president?" Patty suggested, "or just a class mutiny?"

"It 's about Olivia Copeland," Lady Clara returned dubiously; "but I don't know that I ought to say anything."

"Olivia Copeland?" Patty straightened up with a new interest in her eyes. "What 's Olivia Copeland been doing?"

"She 's been flunking and—"

"Flunking!" Patty's face was blank. "But I thought she was so bright!"

"Oh, she is bright; only, you know, she has n't a way of making people find it out; and, besides," Lady Clara added with meaning emphasis, "she was scared over examinations."

Patty cast a quick look at her. "What do you mean?" she asked.

Lady Clara was fond of Patty, but she was only human, and she had been frightened herself. "Well," she explained, "she had heard a lot of stories from—er—upper-classmen about how hard the examinations are, and the awful things they do to you if you don't pass, and being a stranger, she believed them. Of course Emily and I knew better; but she was just scared to death, and she went all to pieces, and—"

"Nonsense!" said Patty, impatiently. "You can't make me believe that."

"If it had been a sophomore that had tried to frighten us," pursued Lady Clara, "we should n't have minded so much; but a senior!"

"Now, Patty, are n't you sorry that you told us all those things?" asked Emily.

Patty laughed. "For the matter of that, I never say anything I 'm not sorry for half an hour later. I 'm going to get out a book some day entitled 'Things I Wish I Had n't Said: A Collection of Faux Pas,' by Patty Wyatt."

"I think it 's more than a faux pas when you frighten a girl so she—"

"I suppose you think you 're rubbing it in," said Patty, imperturbably; "but girls don't flunk because they 're frightened: they flunk because they don't know."

"Olivia knew five times as much geometry as I did, and I got through and she did n't."

Patty examined the carpet in silence.

"She thinks she 's going to be dropped, and she 's just crying terribly," pursued Emily, with a certain relish in the details.

"Crying!" said Patty, sharply. "What 's she crying for?"

"Because she feels bad, I suppose. She 'd been out walking, and got caught in the rain, and she did n't get back in time for dinner, and then found those notes waiting for her. She 's up there lying on the bed, and she 's got hysterics or Roman fever or something like that. She told us to go away and let her alone. She 's awfully cross all of a sudden."

Patty rose. "I think I 'll go and cheer her up."

"Let her alone, Patty," said Emily. "I know the way you cheer people up. If you had n't cheered her up before examinations she would n't have flunked."

"I did n't know anything about her then," said Patty, a trifle sulkily; "and, anyway," she added as she opened the door, "I did n't say anything that affected her passing, one way or the other." She turned toward Olivia's room, however, with a conscience that was not quite comfortable. She could not remember just what she had told those freshmen about examinations, but she had an uneasy feeling that it might not have been of a reassuring nature.

"I wish I could ever learn when it is time for joking and when it is not," she said to herself as she knocked on the study door.

No one answered, and she turned the knob and entered. A stifled sob came from one of the bedrooms, and Patty hesitated.

She was not in the habit of crying herself, and she always felt uncomfortable when other people did it. Something must be done, however, and she advanced to the threshold and silently regarded Olivia, who was stretched face downward on the bed. At the sound of Patty's step she raised her head and cast a startled glance at the intruder, and then buried her face in the pillows again. Patty scribbled an "engaged" sign and pinned it on the study door, and drawing up a chair beside the bed, she sat down with the air of a physician about to make a diagnosis.

"Well, Olivia," she began in a business-like tone, "what is the trouble?"

Olivia opened her hands and disclosed some crumpled papers. Patty spread them out and hastily ran her eyes over the official printed slips:

Miss Copeland is hereby informed that she has been found deficient in German (three hours).

Miss Copeland is hereby informed that she has been found deficient in Latin prose (one hour).

Miss Copeland is hereby informed that she has been found deficient in geometry (four hours).

Patty performed a rapid calculation,– "three and one are four and four are eight,"–and knit her brows.

"Will they send me home, Patty?"

"Mercy, no, child; I hope not. A person who 's done as good work as you in English ought to have the right to flunk every other blessed thing, if she wants to."

"But you 're dropped if you flunk eight hours; you told me so yourself."

"Don't believe anything I told you," said Patty, reassuringly. "I don't know what I 'm talking about more than half the time."

"I 'd hate to be sent back, and have my father know I 'd failed, when he spent so much time preparing me; but"–Olivia began to cry again–"I want to go back so much that I don't believe I care."

"You don't know what you 're talking about," said Patty. She put her hand on the girl's shoulder. "Mercy, child, you 're sopping wet, and you 're shivering! Sit up and take those shoes off."

Olivia sat up and pulled at the laces with ineffectual fingers, and Patty jerked them open and dumped the shoes in a squashy heap on the floor.

"Do you know what 's the matter with you?" she asked. "You 're not crying because you 've flunked. You 're crying because you 've caught cold, and you 're tired and wet and hungry. You take those wet clothes off this minute and get into a warm bath-robe, and I 'll get you some dinner."

"I don't want any dinner," wailed Olivia, and she showed signs of turning back to the pillows again.

"Don't act like a baby, Olivia," said Patty, sharply; "sit up and be a–a man."

Ten minutes later Patty returned from a successful looting expedition, and deposited her spoils on the bedroom table. Olivia sat on the edge of the bed and watched her apathetically, a picture of shivering despondency.

"Drink this," commanded Patty, as she extended a steaming glass.

Olivia obediently raised it to her lips, and drew back. "What 's in it?" she asked faintly.

"Everything I could find that 's hot–quinine and whisky and Jamaica ginger and cough syrup and a dash of red pepper, and–one or two other things. It 's my own idea. You can't take cold after that."

"I–I don't believe I want any."

"Drink it–every drop,"said Patty, grimly; and Olivia shut her eyes and gulped it down.

"Now," said Patty, cheerfully bustling about, "I 'll get dinner. Have you a can-opener? And any alcohol, by chance? That 's nice. We 'll have three courses,–canned soup, canned baked beans, and preserved ginger,–all of them hot. It 's mighty lucky Georgie Merriles was in New York or she 'd never have lent them to me."

Olivia, to her own astonishment, presently found herself laughing (she had thought that she would never smile again) as she sipped mulligatawny soup from a tooth-mug and balanced a pin-trayful of steaming baked beans on her knee.

"And now." said Patty, as, the three courses disposed of, she tucked the freshman into bed, "we 'll map out a campaign. While eight hours are pretty serious, they are not of necessity deadly. What made you flunk Latin prose?"

"I never had any before I came, and when I told Miss– "

"Certainly; she thought it her duty to flunk you. You should n't have mentioned the subject. But never mind. It 's only one hour, and it won't take you a minute to work it off. How about German?"

"German 's a little hard because it 's so different from Italian and French, you know; and I 'm sort of frightened when she calls on me, and–"

"Pretty stupid, on the whole?" Patty suggested.

"I 'm afraid I am," she confessed.

"Well, I dare say you deserved to flunk in that. You can tutor it up and pass it off in the spring. How about geometry?"

"I thought I knew that, only she did n't ask what I expected and–"

"An unfortunate circumstance, but it will happen. Could you review it up a little and take a reëxamination right away?"

"Yes; I 'm sure I could, only they won't give me another chance. They 'll send me home first."

"Who 's your instructor?"

"Miss Prescott."

Patty frowned, and then she laughed.

"I thought if it were Miss Hawley I could go to her and explain the matter and ask her to give you a reëxamination. Miss Hawley 's occasionally human. But Miss Prescott! No wonder you flunked. I 'm afraid of her myself. She 's the only woman that ever got a degree at some German university, and she simply has n't a thought in the world beyond mathematics. I don't believe the woman has any soul. If one of those mediums should come here and dematerialize her, all that would be left would be an equilateral triangle."

Patty shook her head. "I 'm afraid there 's not much use in arguing with a person like that. If she once sees a truth, you know, she sees it for all time. But never mind; I 'll do the best I can. I 'll tell her you 're an undiscovered mathematical genius; that it 's latent, but if she 'll examine you again she 'll find it. That ought to appeal to her. Good-night. Go to sleep and don't worry; I 'll manage her."

"Good night; and thank you, Patty," called a tolerably cheerful voice from under the covers.

Patty closed the door, and stood a moment in the hall, pondering the situation. Olivia Copeland was too valuable to throw away. The college must be made to realize her worth. But that was difficult. Patty had tried to make the college realize things before. Miss Prescott was the only means of salvation that she could think of, and Miss Prescott was a doubtful means. She did not at all relish the prospect of calling on her, but there seemed to be nothing else to do. She made a little grimace and laughed. "I 'm acting like a freshman myself," she thought. "Walk up, Patty, and face the guns"; and without giving herself time to hesitate she

74

marched up-stairs and knocked on Miss Prescott's door. She reflected after she had knocked that perhaps it would have been more politic to have postponed her business until the morrow. But the door opened before she had time to run away, and she found herself rather confusedly bowing to Miss Prescott, who held in her hand, not a book on calculus, but a common, every-day magazine.

"Good evening, Miss Wyatt. Won't you come in and sit down?" said Miss Prescott, in a very cordially human tone.

As she sank into a deep rush chair Patty had a blurred vision of low bookcases, pictures, rugs, and polished brass thrown into soft relief by a shaded lamp which stood on the table. Before she had time to mentally shake herself and reconstruct her ideas she was gaily chatting to Miss Prescott about the probable outcome of a serial story in the magazine.

Miss Prescott did not seem to wonder in the least at this unusual visit, but talked along easily on various subjects, and laughed and told stories like the humanest of human beings. Patty watched her, fascinated. "She 's pretty," she thought to herself, and she began to wonder how old she was. Never before had she associated any age whatever with Miss Prescott. She had regarded her much in the same light as a scientific truth, which exists, but is quite irrespective of time or place. She tried to recall some story that had been handed about among the girls her freshman year. She remembered vaguely that it had in it the suggestion that Miss Prescott had once been in love. At the time Patty had scoffingly repudiated the idea, but now she was half willing to believe it.

Suddenly, in the midst of the conversation, the ten-o'clock bell rang, and Patty recalled her errand with a start.

"I suppose," she said, "you are wondering why I came."

"I was hoping," said Miss Prescott, with a smile, "that it was just to see me, without any ulterior motive."

"It will be the next time–if you will let me come again; but to-night I had another reason, which I 'm afraid you 'll think impertinent– and," she added frankly, "I don't know just what 's the best way to tell it so that you won't think it impertinent."

"Tell it to me any way you please, and I will try not to think so," said Miss Prescott, kindly.

"Don't you think sometimes the girls can tell more of one another's ability than the instructors?" Patty asked. "I know a girl," she continued, "a freshman, who is, in some ways, the most remarkable person I have ever met. Of course I can't be sure, but I should say that she is going to be very good in English some day–so good, you know, that the college will be proud of her. Well, this girl has flunked such a lot that I am afraid she is in danger of being sent home, and the college simply can't afford to lose her. I don't know anything about your rules, of course, but what seems to me the easiest way is for you to give her another examination in geometry immediately,–she really knows it,–and then tell the faculty about her and urge them to give her another trial."

Patty brought out this astounding request in the most matter-of-fact way possible, and the corners of Miss Prescott's mouth twitched as she asked: "Of whom are you speaking?"

"Olivia Copeland."

Miss Prescott's mouth grew firm, and she looked like the instructor in mathematics again.

"Miss Copeland did absolutely nothing on her examination, Miss Wyatt, and what little she has recited during the year does not betoken any unusual ability. I am sorry, but it would be impossible."

"But, Miss Prescott," Patty expostulated, "the girl has worked under such peculiar disadvantages. She 's an American, but she lives abroad, and all our ways are new to her. She has never been to school a day in her life. Her father prepared her for college, and, of course, not in the same way that the other girls have been prepared. She is shy, and not being used to reciting in a class, she does n't know how to show off. I am sure, Miss Prescott, that if you would take her and examine her yourself, you would find that she understands the work–that is, if you would let her get over being afraid of you first. I know you 're busy, and it 's asking a good deal," Patty finished apologetically.

Olivia Copeland

"It is not that, Miss Wyatt, for of course I do not wish to mark any student unjustly; but I cannot help feeling that you have overestimated Miss Copeland's ability. She has really had a chance to show what is in her, and if she has failed in as many courses as you say– The college, you know, must keep up the standard of its work, and in questions like this it is not always possible to consider the individual."

Patty felt that she was being dismissed, and she groped about wildly for a new plea. Her eye caught a framed picture of the old monastery of Amalfi hanging over the bookcase.

"Perhaps you 've lived in Italy?" she asked.

Miss Prescott started slightly. "No," she said; "but I 've spent some time there."

"That picture of Amalfi, up there, made me think of it. Olivia Copeland, you know, lives near there, at Sorrento."

A gleam of interest flashed into Miss Prescott's eye.

"That's how I first came to notice her," continued Patty; "but she did n't interest me so much until I talked to her. It seems that her father is an artist, and she was born in Italy, and has only visited America once when she was a little girl. Her mother is dead, and she and her father live in an old villa on that road along the coast leading to Sorrento. She has never had any girl friends; just her father's friends–artists and diplomats and people like that. She speaks Italian, and she knows all about Italian art and politics and the church and the agrarian laws and how the people are taxed; and all the peasants around Sorrento are her friends. She is so homesick that she nearly dies, and the only person here that she can talk to about the things she is interested in is the peanut man down-town.

"The girls she rooms with are just nice exuberant American girls, and are interested in golf and basket-ball and Welsh rabbit and Richard Harding Davis stories and Gibson pictures–and she never even heard of any of them until four months ago. She has a water-color sketch of the villa, that her father did. It 's white stucco, you know, with terraces and marble balustrades and broken statues, and a grove of ilex-trees with a fountain in the center. Just think of belonging to a place like that, Miss Prescott, and then being suddenly plunged into a place like this without any friends or any one who even knows about the things you know–think how lonely you would be!"

Patty leaned forward with flushed cheeks, carried away by her own eloquence. "You know what Italy 's like. It 's a sort of disease. If you once get fond of it you 'll never forget it, and you just can't be happy till you get back. And with Olivia it 's her home, besides. She 's never known anything else. And it 's hard at first to keep your mind on mathematics when you 're dreaming all the time of ilex groves and fountains and nightingales and–and things like that."

She finished lamely, for Miss Prescott suddenly leaned back in the shadow, and it seemed to Patty that her face had grown pale and the hand that held the magazine trembled.

Patty flushed uncomfortably and tried to think what she had said. She was always saying things that hurt people's feelings without meaning to. Suddenly that old story from her freshman year flashed into her mind. He had been an artist and had lived in Italy and had died of Roman fever; and Miss Prescott had gone to Germany to study mathematics, and had never cared for anything else since. It sounded rather made up, but it might be true. Had she stumbled on a forbidden subject? she wondered miserably. She had, of course; it was just her way.

The silence was becoming unbearable; she struggled to think of something to say, but nothing came, and she rose abruptly.

"I 'm sorry to have taken so much of your time, Miss Prescott. I hope I have n't bored you. Good night."

Miss Prescott rose and took Patty's hand. "Good night, my dear, and thank you for coming to me. I am glad to know of Olivia Copeland. I will see what can be done about her geometry, and I shall be glad, besides, to know her as–as a friend; for I, too, once cared for Italy."

Patty closed the door softly and tiptoed home through the dim corridors.

"Did you bring the matches?" called a sleepy voice from Priscilla's bedroom.

Patty started. "Oh, the matches!" she laughed. "No; I forgot them."

"I never knew you to accomplish anything yet that you started out to do; Patty Wyatt."

"I 've accomplished something to-night, just the same," Patty retorted, with a little note of triumph in her voice; "but I have n't an idea how I happened to do it," she added frankly to herself.

And she went to bed and fell asleep, quite unaware of how much she had accomplished; for unconsciously she had laid the foundation of a friendship which was to make happy the future of a lonely freshman and an equally lonely instructor.

XI "Local Color"

THE third senior table had discovered a new amusement with which to enlighten the tedium of waiting while Maggie was in the kitchen foraging for food. The game was called "local color," in honor of Patty Wyatt's famous definition in English class, "Local color is that which makes a lie seem truthful." The object of the game was to see who could tell the biggest lie without being found out; and the one rule required that the victims be disillusionized before they left the table.

Patty was the instigator, the champion player, and the final victim of the game. Baron Münchhausen himself would have blushed at some of her creations, and her stories were told with such an air of ingenuous honesty that the most outrageous among them obtained credence.

The game in its original conception may have been innocent enough, but the rule was not always as carefully observed as it should have been, and the most unaccountable scandals began to float about college. The president of "Christians" had been called up for cutting chapel. The shark of the class had flunked her ethics, and even failed to get through on the "re." Cathy Fair was an own cousin of Professor Hitchcock's, and called him "Tommy" to his face. These, and far worse, were becoming public property; and even personal fabrications in regard to the faculty, intended solely for undergraduate consumption, were reaching the ears of the faculty themselves.

One day Patty dropped into an underclassman's room on some committee work, and she found the children, in the manner of their elders, regaling themselves on dainty bits of college gossip.

"I heard the funniest thing about Professor Winters yesterday," piped up a sophomore.

"Tell it to us. What was it?" cried a chorus of voices.

"I 'd like to hear something funny about Professor Winters; he 's the solemnest-looking man I ever saw," remarked a freshman.

"Well," resumed the sophomore, "it seems he was going to get married last week, and the invitations were all out, and the presents all there, when the bride came down with the mumps."

"Really? How funny!" came in a chorus from the delighted auditors.

"Yes–on both sides; and the clergyman had never had it, so the ceremony had to be postponed."

Patty's blood froze. She recognized the tale. It was one of her own offspring, only shorn of its unessential adornments.

"Where in the world did you hear any such absurd thing as that?" she demanded severely.

"I heard Lucille Carter tell it at a fudge party up in Bonnie Connaught's room last night," answered the sophomore, stoutly, sure that the source was a reputable one.

Patty groaned. "And I suppose that every blessed one of that dozen girls has told it to another dozen by this time, and that it 's only bounded by the boundaries of the campus. Well, there 's not a word of truth in it. Lucille Carter does n't know what she is talking about. That 's a likely story, is n't it?" she added with fine scorn. "Does Professor Winters look like a man who 'd ever dare propose to a girl, let alone marry her?" And she stalked out of the room and up to the single where Lucille lived.

"Lucille," said Patty, "what do you mean by spreading that story about Professor Winters's bride's mumps?"

"You told it to me yourself," answered Lucille, with some warmth. She was a believing creature with an essentially literal mind, and she had always been out of her element in the lofty imaginative realms of local color.

"I told it to you!" said Patty, indignantly. "You goose, you don't mean to tell me you believed it? I was just playing local color."

"How should I know that? You told it as if it were true."

"Of course," said Patty; "that 's the game. You would n't have believed me if I had n't."

"But you never said it was n't true. You don't follow the rule."

"I did n't think it was necessary. I never supposed any one would believe any such absurd story as that."

"I don't see how it was my fault."

"Of course it was your fault. You should n't be spreading malicious tales about the faculty; it 's irreverent. The story 's all over college by this time, and Professor Winters has probably heard it himself. He 'll flunk you on the finals to pay for it; see if he does n't." And Patty went home, leaving a conscience-smitten and thoroughly indignant Lucille behind her.

ABOUT a month before the introduction of local color, Patty had entered upon a new activity, which she referred to impartially as "molding public opinion" and "elevating the press." The way of it was this:

The college, which was a modest and retiring institution craving only to be unmolested in its atmosphere of academic calm, had been recently exploited by a sensational newspaper. The fact that none of the stories was true did not mitigate the annoyance. The college was besieged by reporters who had heard rumors and wished to have them corroborated for exclusive publication in the "Censor" or "Advertiser" or "Star." And they would also like a photograph of Miss Bentley as she appeared in the character of Portia; and since she refused to give it to them, they stated their intention of "faking" one, which, they gallantly assured her, would be far homelier than the original.

The climax was reached when Bonnie Connaught was unfortunate enough to sprain her ankle in basket-ball. Something more than a life-size portrait of her, clothed in a masculine-looking sweater, with a basket-ball under her arm, appeared in a New York evening paper, and scareheads three inches high announced in red ink that the champion athlete and most popular society girl in college was at death's door, owing to injuries received in basket-ball.

Bonnie's eminently respectable family descended upon the college in an indignant body for the purpose of taking her home, and were with difficulty soothed by an equally indignant faculty. The alumnæ wrote that in their day such brutal games as basket-ball had not been countenanced, and that they feared the college had deteriorated. Parents wrote that they would remove their daughters from college if they were to be subjected to such publicity; and the poor president was, of course, quite helpless before the glorious American privilege of free speech.

Finally the college hit upon a partially protective measure–that of furnishing its own news; and a regularly organized newspaper corps was formed among the students, with a member of the faculty at the head. The more respectable of the papers were very glad to have a correspondent from the inside whose facts needed no investigation, and the less respectable in due time betook themselves to more fruitful fields of scandal and happily forgot the existence of the college.

Patty, having the reputation of being an "English shark," had been duly empaneled and presented with a local paper. At first she had been filled with a fit sense of the responsibility of the position, and had conscientiously neglected her college work for its sake; but in time the novelty wore off, and her weekly budgets became more and more perfunctory in character.

The choice of Patty for this particular paper perhaps had not been very far-sighted, for the editor wished a column a week of what he designated as "chatty news," whereas it would have been wiser to have given her a city paper which required only a brief statement of important facts. Patty's own tendencies, it must be confessed, had a slightly yellow tinge, and, with a delighted editor egging her on, it was hard for her to suppress her latent love for "local color." The paper, however, had a wide circulation among the faculty, which circumstance tended to have a chastening effect.

The day following Patty's bride-with-the-mumps contretemps with Lucille happened to be Friday, and she was painfully engaged in her weekly molding of public opinion. It had been a barren week, and there was nothing to write about.

She reviewed at length a set of French encyclopedias which had been given to the library, and spoke with enthusiasm of a remarkable collection of jaw-bones of the prehistoric cow which had been presented to the department of paleontology. She gave in full the list of the seventeen girls who had been honored with scholarships, laboriously writing out their full names, with "Miss" attached to each, and the name of the town and the State in its unabbreviated length. And still it only mounted up to ten pages, and it took eighteen of Patty's writing to make a column.

She strolled down to examine the bulletin-board again, and discovered a new notice which she had overlooked before:

Friday, January 17. Professor James Harkner Wallis of the Lick Observatory will lecture in the auditorium, at eight o'clock, upon "Theories of the Sidereal System."

Patty regarded the notice without emotion. It did not look capable of expansion, and she did not feel the remotest interest in the sidereal system. The brief account of the lecturer, however, which was appended to the notice, stated that Professor Wallis was one of the best known of living astronomers, and that he had conducted important original investigations.

"If I knew anything about astronomy," she thought desperately, "I might be able to spread him out over two pages."

An acquaintance of Patty's strolled up to the bulletin-board.

"Did you ever hear of that man?" asked Patty, pointing to the notice.

"Never; but I 'm not an astronomer."

"I 'm not, either," said Patty. "I wonder who he is?" she added wistfully. "It seems he 's very famous, and I 'd really like to know something about him."

The girl opened her eyes in some surprise at this thirst for gratuitous information; it did not accord with Patty's reputation: and ever after, when it was affirmed in her presence that Patty Wyatt was brilliant but superficial, she stoutly maintained that Patty was deeper than people thought. She pondered a moment, and then returned, "Lucille Carter takes astronomy; she could tell you about him."

"So she does. I 'd forgotten it"; and Patty swung off toward Lucille's room.

She found a number of girls sitting around on the various pieces of furniture, eating fudge and discussing the tragedies of one Maeterlinck.

"What 's this?" said Patty. "A party?"

"Oh, no," said Lucille; "just an extra session of the Dramatic Theory class. Don't be afraid; there 's your room-mate up on the window-seat."

"Hello, Pris. What are you doing here?" said Patty, dipping out some fudge with a spoon. (There had been a disagreement as to how long it should boil.)

"Just paying a social call. What are you doing? I thought you were going to hurry up and get through so you could go down-town to dinner."

"I am," said Patty, vaguely; "but I got lonely."

The conversation drifting off to Maeterlinck again, she seized the opportunity to inquire of Lucille: "Who's this astronomy man that 's going to lecture to-night? He 's quite famous, is n't he?"

"Very," said Lucille. "Professor Phelps has been talking about him every day for the last week."

"Where 's the Lick Observatory, anyway?" pursued Patty. "I can't remember, for the life of me, whether it 's in California or on Pike's Peak."

Lucille considered a moment. "It 's in Dublin, Ireland."

"Dublin, Ireland?" asked Patty, in some surprise. "I could have sworn that it was in California. Are you sure you know where it is, Lucille?"

"Of course I 'm sure. Have n't we been having it for three days steady? California! You must be crazy, Patty. I think you 'd better elect astronomy."

"I know it," said Patty, meekly. "I was going to, but I heard that it was terribly hard, and I thought senior year you have a right to take something a little easy. But, you know, that's the funniest thing about the Lick Observatory, for I really know a lot about it– read an article on it just a little while ago; and I don't know how I got the impression, but I was almost sure it was in the United States. It just shows that you can never be sure of anything."

"No," said Lucille; "it is n't safe."

"Is it connected with Dublin University?" asked Patty.

"I believe so," said Lucille.

"And this astronomy person," continued Patty, warming to her work–"I suppose he 's an Irishman, then."

"Of course," said Lucille. "He 's very noted."

"What 's he done?" asked Patty. "It said on the bulletin-board he 'd made some important discoveries. I suppose, though, they 're frightful technicalities that no one ever heard of."

"Well," said Lucille, considering, "he discovered the rings of Saturn and the Milky Way."

"The rings of Saturn! Why, I thought those had been discovered ages ago. He must be a terribly old man. I remember reading about them when I was an infant in arms."

"It was a good while ago," said Lucille. "Eight or nine years, at least."

"And the Milky Way!" continued Patty, with a show of incredulity. "I don't see how people could have helped discovering that long ago. I could have done it myself, and I don't pretend to know anything about astronomy."

"Oh, of course," Lucille hastened to explain, "the phenomenon had been observed before, but had never been accounted for."

"I see," said Patty, surreptitiously taking notes. "He must really be an awfully important man. How did he happen to do all this?"

"He went up in a balloon," said Lucille, vaguely.

"A balloon! What fun!" exclaimed Patty, her reportorial instinct waking to the scent. "They use balloons a lot more in Europe than they do here."

"I believe he has his balloon with him here in America," said Lucille. "He never travels without it."

"What 's the good of it?" inquired Patty. "I suppose," she continued, furnishing her own explanation, "it gets him such a lot nearer to the stars."

"That 's without doubt the reason," said Lucille.

"I wish he 'd send it up here," sighed Patty. "Do you know any more interesting details about him?"

"N–no," said Lucille; "I can't think of any more at present."

"He 's certainly the most interesting professor I ever heard of," said Patty, "and it 's strange I never heard of him before."

"There seem to be a good many things you have never heard of," observed Lucille.

"Yes," acknowledged Patty; "there are."

"Well, Patty," said Priscilla, emerging from the discussion on the other side of the room, "if you 're going to dinner with me, you 'd better stop fooling with Lucille, and go home and get your work done."

"Very well" sad Patty, rising with obliging promptitude. "Good-by, girls. Come and see me and I 'll give you some fudge that 's done. Thank you for the information," she called back to Lucille.

THE Monday afternoon following, Patty and Priscilla, with two or three other girls, came strolling back from the lake, jingling their skates over their arms.

"Come in, girls, and have some hot tea," said Priscilla, as they reached the study door.

"Here 's a note for Patty," said Bonnie Connaught, picking up an envelop from the table. "Terribly official-looking. Must have come in the college mail. Open it, Patty, and let 's see what you 've flunked."

"Dear me!" said Patty, "I thought that was a habit I 'd outgrown freshman year."

They crowded around and read the note over her shoulder. Patty had no secrets.

THE OBSERVATORY, January 20.

Miss Patty Wyatt.

DEAR MISS WYATT: I am informed that you are the correspondent for the "Saturday Evening Post-Despatch," and I take the liberty of calling your attention to a rather grave error which occurred in last week's issue. You stated that the Lick Observatory is in Dublin, Ireland, while, as is a matter of general information, it is situated near San Francisco, California. Professor James Harkner Wallis is not an Irishman; he is an American. Though he has carried on some very important investigations, he is the discoverer of neither the rings of Saturn nor the Milky Way.

Very truly yours, HOWARD D. PHELPS.

"It 's from Professor Phelps–what can he mean?" said the Twin, in bewilderment.

"Oh, Patty," groaned Priscilla, "you don't mean to say that you actually believed all that stuff?"

"Of course I believed it. How could I know she was lying?"

"She was n't lying. Don't use such reckless language."

"I 'd like to know what you call it, then?" said Patty, angrily.

"Local color, my dear, just local color. The worm will turn, you know."

"Why did n't you tell me?" wailed Patty.

"Never supposed for a moment you believed her. Thought you were joking all the time."

"What 's the matter, Patty? What have you done?" the others demanded, divided between a pardonable feeling of curiosity and a sense that they ought to retire before this domestic tragedy.

"Oh, tell them," said Patty, bitterly. "Tell every one you see. Shout it from the dome of the observatory. You might as well; it 'll be all over college in a couple of hours."

Priscilla explained, and as she explained the funny side began to strike her. By the time she had finished they were all–except Patty–reduced to hysterics.

"The poor editor," gurgled Priscilla. "He 's always after a scoop, and he 's certainly got one this time."

"Where is it, Patty–the paper?" gasped Bonnie.

"I threw it away," said Patty, sulkily.

Priscilla rummaged it out of the waste-basket, and the four bent over it delightedly.

Ireland's eminent astronomer spending a few weeks in America lecturing at the principal colleges–His famous discovery of the rings of Saturn made during a balloon ascension three thousand feet in the air–Though this is his first visit to the States, he speaks with only a slight brogue–Loyal son of old Erin

"Patty, Patty! And you, of all people, to be so gullible!"

"Professor James Harkner Wallis's parents will be writing to Prexy next to say that their son can't lecture here any more if he is to be subjected to this sort of thing."

"It 's disgusting!" said Bonnie Connaught, feelingly.

"When you 've got through laughing, I wish you 'd tell me what to do."

"Tell Professor Phelps it was a slip of the pen."

"A slip of the pen to the extent of half a column is good," said the Twin.

"I think you girls are beastly to laugh when I am probably being expelled this minute."

"Faculty meeting does n't come till four," said Bonnie.

Patty sat down by the desk and buried her head in her arms.

"Patty," said Priscilla, "you are n't crying, are you?"

"No," said Patty, savagely; "I 'm thinking."

"You will never think of anything that will explain that."

Patty looked up with the air of one who has received an inspiration. "I 'm going to tell him the truth."

"Don't do anything so rash," pleaded the Twin.

"That is, of course, the only thing you can do," said Priscilla. "Sit down and write him a note, and I 'll promise not to laugh till you get through."

Patty stood up. "I think," she said, "I 'll go and see him."

"Oh, no. Write him a note. It 's loads easier."

"No," said Patty, with dignity; "I think I owe him a personal explanation. Is my hair all right? If you girls reveal this to a single person before I come back, I 'll not tell you a thing he says," she added as she closed the door.

Patty returned half an hour later, just as they were finally settling down to tea. She peered around the darkening room; finding only four expectant faces, she leisurely seated herself on a cushion on the floor and stretched out her hand for a steaming cup.

"What did he say? What kept you so long?"

"Oh, I stopped in the office to change my electives, and it delayed me."

"You don't mean to tell me that man made you elect astronomy?" Priscilla asked indignantly.

"Certainly not," said Patty. "I should n't have done it if he had."

"Oh, Patty, I know you like to tease, but I think it 's odious. You know we 're in suspense. Tell us what happened."

"Well," said Patty, placidly gathering her skirts about her, "I told him exactly how it was. I did n't hide anything–not even the bride with the mumps."

"Was he cross, or did he laugh?"

"He laughed," said Patty, "till I thought he was going to fall off his chair, and I looked anxiously around for some water and a call-bell. He really has a surprising sense of humor for a member of the faculty."

"Was he nice?"

"Yes," said Patty; "he was a dear. When he got through discussing Universal Truth, I asked him if I might elect astronomy, and he said I would find it pretty hard the second semester; but I told him I was willing to work, and he said I really showed a remarkable aptitude for explaining phenomena, and that if I were in earnest he would be glad to have me in the class."

"I think a man as forgiving as that ought to be elected," said Priscilla.

"You certainly have more courage than I gave you credit for," said Bonnie. "I never could have gone over and explained to that man in the wide world."

Patty smiled discreetly. "When you have to explain to a woman," she said in the tone of one who is stating a natural law, "it is better to write a note; but when it is a man, always explain in person."

XII The Exigencies of Etiquette

IF I had been the one to invent etiquette," said Patty, "I should have made party calls payable one year after date, and then should have allowed three days' grace at the end."

"In which case," said Priscilla, "I suppose you would get out of calling on Mrs. Millard altogether."

"Exactly," said Patty.

Mrs. Millard–more familiarly referred to as Mrs. Prexy–annually invited the seniors to dinner in parties of ten. Patty, whose turn had come a short time before, owing to an untoward misfortune, had been in the infirmary at the time; but, though she had missed the fun, she now found it necessary to pay the call.

"Of course," she resumed, "I can see why you should be expected to call if you attend the function and partake of the food; but what I can't understand is why a peaceable citizen who desires only to gang his ain gait should, upon the reception of an entirely unsolicited invitation, suddenly find it incumbent upon him to put on his best dress and his best hat and gloves in order to call upon people he barely knows."

"Your genders," said Priscilla, "are a trifle mixed."

"That," said Patty, "is the fault of the language. The logic, I think, you will find correct. You can see what would happen," she pursued, "if you carry it out to its logical conclusion. Suppose, for instance, that every woman I have ever met in this town should suddenly take it into her head to invite me to a dinner. Here I–perfectly unsuspicious and innocent of any evil, because of a purely arbitrary law which I did not help to make–would not only have to sit down and write a hundred regrets, but would have to pay a hundred calls within the next two weeks. It makes me shudder to think of it!"

"I don't believe you need worry about it, Patty; of course we know you 're popular, but you 're not as popular as that."

"No," said Patty; "I did n't mean that I thought I really should get that many invitations. It 's only that one is open to the constant danger."

During the progress of this conversation Georgie Merriles had been lounging on the couch by the window, reading the "Merchant of Venice" in a critically unimpassioned way that the instructor in Dramatic Theory could not have praised too much. The room finally having become too dark for reading, she threw down the book with something like a yawn. "It would have been a joke on Portia," she remarked, "if Bassanio had chosen the wrong casket"; and she turned her attention to the campus outside. Groups of girls were coming along the path from the lake, and the sound of their voices, mingled with laughter and the jingling of skates, floated up through the gathering dusk. Across the stretches of snow and bare trees lights were beginning to twinkle in the other dormitories, while nearer at hand, and more clearly visible, rose the irregular outline of the president's house.

"Patty," said Georgie, with her nose against the pane, "if you really want to get that call out of the way, now 's your chance. Mrs. Millard has just gone out."

Patty dashed into her bedroom and began jerking out bureau drawers. "Priscilla," she called in an agonized tone, "do you remember where I keep my cards?"

"It 's ten minutes of six, Patty; you can't go now."

"Yes, I can. It does n't matter what time it is, so long as she 's out. I 'll go just as I am."

"Not in a golf-cape!"

Patty hesitated an instant. "Well," she admitted, "I suppose the butler might tell her. I 'll put on a hat"–this with the air of one who is making a really great concession. Some more banging of bureau drawers, and she appeared in a black velvet hat trimmed with lace, with the brown jacket of her suit over her red blouse, and a blue golf-skirt and very muddy boots showing below.

"Patty, you 're a disgrace to the room!" cried Priscilla. "Do you mean to tell me that you are going to Mrs. Millard's in a short skirt and those awful skating-shoes?"

"The butler won't look at my feet; I 'm so beautiful above"; and Patty banged the door behind her.

Georgie and Priscilla flattened themselves against the window to watch the progress of the call.

"Look," gasped Priscilla. "There 's Mrs. Millard going in at the back door."

"And there 's Patty. My, but she looks funny!"

"Call her back," cried Priscilla, wildly trying to open the window.

"Let her alone," laughed Georgie; "it will be such fun to gloat over her."

The window came up with a jerk. "Patty! Patty!" shrieked Priscilla.

Patty turned and waved her hand airily. "Can't stop now–will be back in a moment"; and she sped on around the corner.

The two stood watching the house for several minutes, vaguely expecting an explosion of some sort to occur. But nothing happened. Patty was swallowed as if by the grave, and the house gave no sign. They accordingly shrugged their shoulders and dressed for dinner with the philosophy which a life fraught with alarms and surprises gives.

DINNER was half over, and the table had finished discussing Patty's demise, when that young lady trailed placidly in, smiled on the expectant faces, and inquired what kind of soup they had had.

"Bean soup; it was n't any good," said Georgie, impatiently. "What happened? Did you have a nice call?"

"No, Maggie, I don't care for any soup to-night. Just bring me some steak, please."

"Patty!" in a pleading chorus, "what happened?"

"Oh, I beg your pardon," said Patty, sweetly. "Yes, thank you, I had a very pleasant call. May I trouble you for the bread, Lucille?"

"Patty, I think you 're obnoxious," said Georgie. "Tell us what happened."

"Well," began Patty, in a leisurely manner, "I said to the butler, 'Is Mrs. Millard in?' and he said to me (without even a smile), 'I am not sure, miss; will you please step into the drawing-room and I 'll see,' I was going to tell him that he need n't bother, as I knew she was out; but I thought that perhaps it would look a little better if I waited and let him find out for himself. So I walked in and sat down in a pink-and-white embroidered Louis-Quatorze chair. There was a big mirror in front of me, and I had plenty of time to study the effect, which, I will acknowledge, was a trifle mixed."

"A trifle," Georgie assented.

"I was beginning," pursued Patty, "to feel nervous for fear some of the family might drop in, when the man came back and said, 'Mrs. Millard will be down in a minute.'

"If I had seen you at that moment, Georgie Merriles, there would have been battle, murder, and sudden death. My first thought was of flight; but the man was guarding the door, and Mrs. Prexy had my card. While I was frenziedly trying to think of a valid excuse for my costume the lady came in, and I rose and greeted her graciously, one might almost say gushingly. I talked very fast and tried to hypnotize her, so that she would keep her eyes on my face; but it was no use: I saw them traveling downward, and pretty soon I knew by the amused expression that they had arrived at my shoes.

"Concealment was no longer possible," pursued Patty, warming to her subject. "I threw myself upon her mercy and confessed the whole damning truth. What kind of ice-cream is that?" she demanded, leaning forward and gazing anxiously after a passing maid. "Don't tell me they 're giving us raspberry again!"

"No; it 's vanilla. Go on, Patty."

"Well, where was I?"

"You 'd just told her the truth."

"Oh, yes. She said she 'd always wanted to meet the college girls informally and know them just as they are, and she was very glad of this opportunity. And there I sat, looking like a kaleidoscope and feeling like a fool, and she taking it for granted that I was being perfectly natural. Complimentary, was n't it? At this point dinner was announced, and she invited me to stay–quite insisted, in fact, to make up, she said, for the one I had missed when I was ill in the infirmary." Patty looked around the table with a reminiscent smile.

"What did you say? Did you refuse?" asked Lucille.

"No; I accepted, and am over there at present, eating pâté de foie gras."

"No, really, Patty; what did you say?"

"Well," said Patty, "I told her that this was ice-cream night at the college, and that I sort of hated to miss it; but that to-morrow would be mutton night, which I did n't mind missing in the least; so if she would just as leave transfer her invitation, I would accept for to-morrow with pleasure."

"Patty," exclaimed Lucille, in a horrified tone, "you did n't say that!"

"Just a little local color, Lucille," laughed Priscilla.

"But," objected Lucille, "we 'd promised not to play local color any more."

"Have you not learned," said Priscilla, "that Patty can no more live without local color than she can live without food? It 's ingrained in her nature."

"Never mind," said Patty, good-naturedly; "you may not believe me now, but to-morrow night, when I 'm all dressed up in beautiful clothes, swapping stories with Prexy and eating lobster salad, while you are over here having mutton, then maybe you 'll be sorry."

XIII A Crash Without

I LOVE the smell of powder," said Patty.

"Gunpowder or baking-powder?"

As Patty at the moment had her nose buried in a box of face-powder she thought it unnecessary to answer.

"It brings back my youth," she pursued. "The best times of my life have been mixed up with powder and rouge–Washington's Birthday nights and minstrel shows, and masquerades, and plays at boarding-school, and even Mother Goose tableaux when I was a–"

Patty's reminiscences were interrupted by Georgie, who was anxiously pacing up and down the wings. "It 's queer some of the cast don't come. I told them to be here early, so we could get them all made up and not have a rush at the end."

"Oh, there 's time enough," said Patty, comfortably. "It is n't seven yet, and if they 're going to dress in their rooms it won't take any time over here just to make them up and put on their wigs. It 's a comparatively small cast, you see. Now, on the night of the Trig ceremonies, when we had to make up three whole ballets and only had one box of make-up, we were rushed. I thought I 'd never live to see the curtain go down. Do you remember the suit of chain-mail we made for Bonnie Connaught out of wire dish-cloths? It took sixty-three, and the ten-cent store was terribly dubious about renting them to us; and then, after working every spare second for three days over the thing, we found, the last minute, that we had n't left a big enough hole for her to get into, and–"

"Oh, do keep still, Patty," said Georgie, nervously; "I can't remember what I have to do when you talk all the time."

A manager on the eve of producing a new play, with his reputation at stake, may be excused for being a trifle irritable. Patty merely shrugged her shoulders and descended through the stage-door to the half-lighted hall, where she found Cathy Fair strolling up and down the center aisle in an apparently aimless manner.

"Hello, Cathy," said Patty; "what are you doing over here?"

"I 'm head usher, and I wanted to see if those foolish sophomores had mixed up the numbers again."

"It strikes me they 're a trifle close together," said Patty, sitting down and squeezing in her knees.

"Yes, I know; but you can't get eight hundred people into this hall any other way. When we once get them packed they 'll have to sit still, that 's all. What are you doing over here yourself?" she continued. "I did n't know you were on the committee. Or are you just helping Georgie?"

"I 'm in the cast," said Patty.

"Oh, are you? I saw the program to-day, but I 'd forgotten it. I 've often wondered why you have n't been in any of the class plays."

"Fortune and the faculty are against it," sighed Patty. "You see, they did n't discover my histrionic ability before examinations freshman year, and after examinations, when I was asked to be in the play, the faculty thought I could spend the time to better advantage studying Greek. At the time of the sophomore play I was on something else and could n't serve, and this year I had just been deprived of my privileges for coming back late after Christmas."

"But I thought you said you were in it?"

"Oh," said Patty, "it 's a minor part, and my name does n't appear."

"What sort of a part is it?"

"I 'm a crash."

"A crash?"

"Yes, 'a crash without.' Lord Bromley says, 'Cynthia, I will brave all for your sake. I will follow you to the ends of the earth.' At this point a crash is heard without. I," said Patty, proudly, "am the crash. I sit behind a moonlit balcony in a space about two feet square, and drop a lamp-chimney into a box. It may not sound like a very important part, but it is the pivot upon which the whole plot turns."

"I hope you won't be taken with stage-fright," laughed Cathy.

"I 'll try not," said Patty. "There comes the butler and Lord Bromley and Cynthia. I 've got to go and make them up."

"Why are you making people up, if you are not on the committee?"

"Oh, once, during a period of mental weakness, I took china-painting lessons, and I 'm supposed to know how. Good-by."

"Good-by. If you get any flowers I 'll send them in by an usher."

"Do," said Patty. "I 'm sure to get a lot."

Behind the scenes all was joyful confusion. Georgie, in a short skirt, with her shirt-waist sleeves rolled up and a notebook in her hand, was standing in the middle of the stage directing the scene-shifters and distracted committee. Patty, in the "green-room," was presiding over the cast, with a hare's foot in one hand and the other daubed with red and blue grease-paints.

"Oh, Patty," remonstrated Cynthia, with a horrified glance in the mirror, "I look more like a soubrette than a heroine."

"That 's the way you ought to look," returned Patty. "Here, hold still till I put another dab on your chin."

Cynthia appealed to the faithful Lord Bromley, who was sitting in the background, politely letting the ladies go first. "Look, Bonnie, don't you think I 'm too red? I know it 'll all come off when you kiss me."

"If it comes off as easily as that, you 'll be more fortunate than most of the people I make up"; and Patty smiled knowingly as she remembered how Priscilla had soaked half the night on the occasion of a previous play, and then had appeared at breakfast the next morning with lowering eyebrows and a hectic flush on each cheek. "You must remember that footlights take a lot of color," she explained condescendingly. "You 'd look ghastly if I let you go the way you wanted to at first. Next!"

"No," said Patty, as the butler presented himself; "you don't come till the second act. I 'll take the Irate Parent first." The Irate Parent was dragged from a corner where he had been anxiously mumbling over his lines. "What 's the matter?" asked Patty, as she began daubing in wrinkles with a liberal hand; "are you afraid?"

"N-no," said the Parent; "I 'm not afraid, only I 'm afraid that I will be afraid."

"You 'd just better change your mind, then," said Patty, sternly. "We are n't going to allow any stage-fright to-night."

"Patty, you can manage Georgie Merriles; make her let me go on without any wig," cried Cynthia, returning and holding up to view a mass of yellow curls of a shade that was never produced in the course of nature.

Patty looked at the wig critically. "It is, perhaps, a trifle golden for the part."

"Golden!" said Cynthia. "It 's positively orange. Wait till you see how it lights up. He calls me his dark-eyed beauty: and I 'm sure no one with dark eyes, or any other kind of eyes, would have hair like that. My own looks a great deal better."

"Why don't you wear your own, then? Wrinkle up your forehead, Parent, and let me see which way they run."

"Georgie paid two dollars for renting it, and she 's bound to get the money's worth of wear out of it, even if she makes me look like a fright and spoils the play."

"Nonsense," said Patty, pushing away the Parent and giving her undivided attention to the question. "Your own hair does look better. Just mislay the wig and keep out of Georgie's way till the curtain goes up. The audience are beginning to come," she announced to the room in general, "and you 've got to keep still back there. You re making an awful racket, and they can hear you all over the house. Here, what are you making such a noise for?" she demanded of Lord Bromley, who came clumping up with footfalls which reverberated through the flies.

"I can't help it," he said crossly. "Look at these boots. They 're so big that I can step out of them without unlacing them."

"It 's not my fault. I have n't anything to do with the costumes."

"I know it; but what can I do?"

"Never mind," said Patty, soothingly; "they don't look so awfully bad. You 'll have to try and walk without raising your feet."

She went out on the stage, where Georgie was giving her last directions to the scene-shifters. "The minute the curtain goes down on the first act change this forest to the drawing-room scene, and don't make any noise hammering. If you have to hammer, do it while the orchestra 's playing. How does it look?" she asked anxiously, turning to Patty.

"Beautiful," said Patty. "I 'd scarcely recognize it."

The "forest scene" had served in every outdoor capacity for the last four years, and it was usually hailed with a groan on the part of the audience.

"I was just coming in to see if the cast were ready," said Georgie.

"They 're all made up, and are sitting in the green-room getting stage-fright. What shall I do now?"

"Let me see," said Georgie, consulting her book. "One of the committee is to prompt, one is to stay with the men and see that they manage the curtain and the lights in the right places, one is to give the cues, and two are to help change costumes. Cynthia has to change from a riding-habit to a ball-gown in four minutes. I think you 'd better help her, too."

"Anything you please," said Patty, obligingly. "I 'll stand on a stool with the ball-gown in the air ready to drop it over her head the moment she appears, like a harness on a fire-horse. Is everything out here done? What time is it?"

"Yes; everything 's done, and it 's five minutes of eight. We can begin as soon as the audience is ready."

They peered through the folds of the heavy velvet curtain at the sea of faces in front. Eight hundred girls in light evening-gowns were talking and laughing and singing. Snatches of song would start up in one corner and sweep gaily over the house, and sometimes two would meet and clash in the center, to the horror of those who preferred harmony to volume.

"Here come the old girls!" said Patty, as a procession of some fifty filed into reserved seats near the front. "There are loads of last year's class back. What are the juniors doing? Look; I believe they are going to serenade them."

The juniors rose in a body, and, turning to their departed sister class, sang a song notable for its sentiment rather than its meter.

"I do hope it will be a success," sighed Georgie. "If it does n't come up to last year's senior play I shall die."

"Oh, it will," said Patty, reassuringly. "Anything would be better than that."

"Now the glee club 's going to sing two songs," said Georgie. "Thank heaven, they 're new!" she added fervently. "And the orchestra plays an overture, and then the curtain goes up. Run and tell them to come out here, ready for the first act."

Lord Bromley was standing in the wings disgustedly viewing the banquet-table. "See here, Patty," he called as she hurried past. "Look at this stuff Georgie Merriles has palmed off on us for wine. You can't expect me to drink any such dope as that."

Patty paused for an instant. "What 's the matter with it?" she inquired, pouring out some in a glass and holding it up to the light.

"Matter? It 's made of currant jelly and water, with cold tea mixed in."

"I made it myself," said Patty, with some dignity. "It 's a beautiful color."

"But I have to drain my glass at a draught," expostulated the outraged lord.

"I 'm sure there 's nothing in currant jelly or tea to hurt you. You can be thankful it is n't poisonous." And Patty hurried on.

The glee club sang the two new songs, punctuated with the appreciative applause of a long-suffering audience, and the orchestra commenced the overture.

"Everybody clear the stage," said Georgie, in a low tone, "and you keep your eyes on the book," she added sternly to the prompter; "you lost your place twice at the dress rehearsal."

The overture died down; a bell tinkled, and the curtain parted in the middle, discovering Cynthia sitting on a garden-seat in the castle park (originally the Forest of Arden).

As the curtain fell at the end of the act, and the applause gave way to an excited buzz in the audience, Patty hugged Georgie gleefully. "It 's fifty times better than last year!"

"Heaven send Theo Granby is out there!" piously ejaculated Georgie. (Theo Granby had been the chairman of last year's senior play.)

THE curtain had risen on the fourth act, and Patty squeezed herself into the somewhat close quarters behind the balcony. There was fortunately—or rather unfortunately—a window in the rear of the building at this point, and Patty opened it and perched herself at one end of the sill, with the lamp-chimney ready for use at the other end. The crash was not due for some time, and Patty, having lately elected astronomy, whiled away the interval by examining the stars.

On the stage matters were approaching a climax. Lord Bromley was making an excellent lover, as was proved by the fact that the audience was taking him seriously instead of laughing through the love scenes as usual.

"Cynthia," he implored, "say that you will be mine, and I will brave all for your sake. I will follow you to the ends of the earth." He gazed tenderly into her eyes, and waited for the crash. A silence as of the tomb prevailed, and he continued to gaze tenderly, while a grin rapidly spread over the audience.

"Hang Patty!" he murmured savagely. "Might have known she 'd do something like this.–What was that? Did you hear a noise?" he asked aloud.

"No," said Cynthia, truthfully; "I did not hear anything."

"Pretend you did," he whispered, and they continued to improvise. After some five minutes of hopeless floundering, the prompter got them back on the track again, and the act proceeded, with the audience happily unaware that anything was missing. ➤

Ten minutes later Lord Bromley was declaiming: "Cynthia, let us flee this place. Its dark rooms haunt me; its silence oppresses me–" And the crash came.

For the first moment the audience was too startled to notice that the actors were also taken by surprise. Then Lord Bromley, who was getting used to emergencies, pulled himself together and ejaculated, "Hark! What was that sound?"

"I think it was a crash," said Cynthia.

He grasped her hand and ran back toward the balcony. "Give us our lines," he said to the prompter, as he went past.

The prompter had dropped the book, and could n't find the place.

"Make them up," came in a piercing whisper from behind the balcony.

A silence ensued while the two dashed back and forth, looking excitedly up and down the stage. Then the despairing Lord Bromley stretched out his arms in a gesture of supplication. "Cynthia," he burst out in tones of realistic longing, "I cannot bear this horrible suspense. Let us flee." And they fled, fully three pages too early, forgetting to leave the letter which should have apprised the Irate Parent of the circumstance.

Georgie was tramping up and down the wings, wringing her hands and lamenting the day that ever Patty had been born.

"Hurry up that Parent before they stop clapping," said Lord Bromley, "and they 'll never know the difference."

The poor old man, with his wig over one ear, was unceremoniously hustled on to the stage, where he raved up and down and swore never to forgive his ungrateful daughter in so realistic a manner that the audience forgot to wonder how he found it out. In due time the runaways returned from the notary's, overcame the old man's harshness, received the parental blessing, and the curtain fell on a scene of domestic felicity that delighted the freshmen in the gallery.

Patty crawled out from under the balcony and fell on her knees at Georgie's feet.

Lord Bromley raised her up. "Never mind, Patty. The audience does n't know the difference; and, anyway, it was all for the best. My mustache would n't have stayed on more than two minutes longer."

They could hear some one shouting in the front, "What 's the matter with Georgie Merriles?" and a hundred voices replied, "She 's all right!"

"Who 's all right?"

"G-e-o-r-g-i-e M-e-r-r-i-l-e-s."

"What 's the matter with the cast?"

"They 're all right!"

The stage-door burst open and a crowd of congratulatory friends burst in and gathered around the disheveled actors and committee. "It 's the best senior play since we 've been in college." "The freshmen are simply crazy over it." "Lord Bromley, your room will be full of flowers for a month." "Patty," called the head usher, over the heads of the others, "let me congratulate you. I was in the very back of the room, and never heard a thing but your crash. It sounded fine!"

"Patty," demanded Georgie, "what in the world were you doing?"

"I was counting the stars," said the contrite Patty, "and then I remembered too late, and I turned around suddenly, and it fell off. I am terribly sorry."

"Never mind," laughed Georgie; "since it turned out well, I 'll forgive you. All the cast and committee," she said, raising her voice, "come up to my room for food. I 'm sorry I can't invite you all," she added to the girls crowded in the doorway, "but I live in a single."

XIV The Mystery Of The Shadowed Sophomore

OH, I say, Bonnie– Bonnie Connaught! Priscilla! Wait a minute," called a girl from across the links, as the two were strolling homeward one afternoon, dragging their caddie-bags behind them. They turned and waited while Bonnie's sophomore cousin, Mildred Connaught, dashed up. She grasped them excitedly, and at the same time glanced over her shoulder with the air of a criminal who is being tracked.

"I want to tell you something," she panted. "Come in here where no one will see us"; and she dived into a clump of pine-trees growing by the path. Priscilla and Bonnie followed more leisurely, and dropped down on the soft needles with an air of amused tolerance.

"Well, Mildred, what 's the matter?" Bonnie inquired mildly.

The sophomore lowered her voice to an impressive whisper, although there was not a person within a hundred yards. "I am being followed," she said solemnly.

"Followed!" exclaimed Bonnie, in amazement. "Are you crazy, child? You act like a boy who 's been reading dime novels."

"Listen, girls. You must n't tell a soul, because it 's a great secret, We 're going to plant the class tree to-night, and I am chairman of the ceremonies. Everything is ready–the costumes are finished and the plans all arranged so that the class can get out to the place without being seen. The freshmen have n't a suspicion that it 's going to be to-night. But they have found out that I 'm chairman of the committee, and, if you please,"–Mildred's eyes grew wide with excitement,–"they 've been tracking me for a week. They have relays of girls appointed to watch me, and I can't stir without a freshman tagging along behind. When I went down to order the ice-cream, there was one right at my elbow, and I had to pretend that I 'd come for soda-water. I have simply had to let the rest of the committee do all of the work, because I was so afraid the freshmen would find out the time. It was funny at first, but I am getting nervous. It 's horrible to think that you 're being watched all the time. I feel as if I 'd committed a murder, and keep looking over my shoulder like–like Macbeth."

"It 's awful," Bonnie shuddered. "I 'm thrilled to the bone to think of the peril a member of my family is braving for the sake of her class."

"You need n't laugh," said Mildred. "It 's a serious matter. If those freshmen come to our tree ceremonies, we 'll never hear the last of it. But they are not going to come," she added with a meaning smile. "They have another engagement. We chose to-night because there 's a lecture before the Archæological Society by some alumna person who 's been digging up remains in Rome. The freshmen have been told to go and hear her on account of their Latin. Imagine their feelings when they are cooped up in the auditorium, trying to look intelligent about the Roman Forum, and listening to our yells outside!"

Priscilla and Bonnie smiled appreciatively. It was not so long, after all, since they themselves were sophomores, and they recalled their own tree ceremonies, when the freshmen had not been cooped up.

"But the trouble is," pursued Mildred, "that it 's more important for me to get there than any one else, because I have to dig the hole,–Peters is really going to dig it, you know; I just take out the first shovelful,–but I can't get there on account of that beastly scout. As soon as she saw me acting suspicious, she 'd run and warn the class."

"I see," said Bonnie; "but what have Priscilla and I to do with it?"

"Well," said Mildred, tentatively, "you 're both pretty big, you know, and you 're our sister class, and you ought to help us."

"Certainly," acquiesced Bonnie; "but in just what way?"

"Well, my idea was this. If you would just stroll down by the lake after chapel, and loiter sort of inconspicuously among the trees, you know, I would come that way a little later, and then, when the detective person came along after me, you could just nab her and–"

"Chuck her in the lake?" asked Bonnie.

"No, of course not. Don't use any force. Just politely detain her till you hear us yelling–take her for a walk. She 'd feel honored."

Bonnie laughed. The program struck her as entertaining. "I don't see anything very immoral in delaying a freshman who is going where she has no business to go. What do you say, Pris?"

"It 's not exactly a Sunday-school excursion," acknowledged Priscilla, "but I don't see why it is n't as legitimate for us to play detective as for them."

"By all means," said Bonnie. "Behold Sherlock Holmes and his friend Dr. Watson about to solve the Mystery of the Shadowed Sophomore."

"You 've saved my life," said Mildred, feelingly. "Don't forget. Right after chapel, by the lake." She peered warily out through the branches. "I 've got to get the keys to the gymnasium, so the refreshments can be put in during chapel. Do you see anybody lurking about? I guess I can get off without being seen. Good-by"; and she sped away like a hunted animal.

Bonnie looked after her and laughed. "'Youth is a great time, but somewhat fussy,'" she quoted; and the two took their homeward way.

They found Patty, who was experiencing a periodical fit of studying, immersed in dictionaries and grammars. It was under protest that she allowed herself to be interrupted long enough to hear the story of their proposed adventure.

"You babies!" she exclaimed. "Have n't you grown up yet? Don't you think it 's a little undignified for seniors–one might almost say alumnæ–to be kidnapping freshmen?"

"We 're not kidnapping freshmen," Bonnie remonstrated; "we 're teaching them manners. It 's my duty to protect my little cousin."

"You can come with us and help detect," said Priscilla, generously.

"Thank you," said Patty, loftily. "I have n't time to play with you children. Cathy Fair and I are going to do Old English to-night."

That evening, as Patty, keyed to the point of grappling with and throwing whole pages of "Beowulf," stood outside the chapel door waiting for Cathy to appear, the professor of Latin came out with a stranger.

"Oh, Miss Wyatt!" she exclaimed in a relieved tone, pouncing upon Patty. "I wish to present you to Miss Henderson, one of our alumnæ who is to lecture to-night before the Archæological Society. She has not been back for several years, and wishes to see the new buildings. Have you time to show her around the campus a little before the lecture begins?"

Patty bowed and murmured that she would be most happy, and cast an agonized glance back at Cathy as she led the lecturer off. As they strolled about, Patty poured out all the statistics she knew about the various buildings, and Miss Henderson received them with exclamations of delighted surprise. She was rather young and gushing for a Ph.D. and an archæologist, Patty decided, and she wondered desperately how she could dispose of her and get back to "Beowulf" and Cathy.

They rounded the top of a little hill, and Miss Henderson exclaimed delightedly, "There is the lake, just as it used to be!"

Patty stifled a desire to remark that lakes had a habit of staying where they used to be, and asked politely if Miss Henderson would like to take a row.

Miss Henderson thought that it would be pleasant; but she had forgotten her watch, and was afraid there would not be time.

Patty glanced about vaguely for some further object of interest, and spied Mildred Connaught sauntering toward the lake. She had forgotten all about the Sherlock Holmes adventure, and she suddenly had an inspiration. Be it said to her credit that she hesitated a moment; but the lecturer's next remark led to her own undoing. She was murmuring something about feeling like a stranger, and wishing that she might know the students informally and see a little of the real college life.

"It would be a pity not to gratify her when I can do it so easily," Patty told herself; and she added out loud, "I am sure we have time for a little row, Miss Henderson. You walk on, and I will run back and get my watch; it won't take a minute."

"I would n't have you do that; it is too much trouble," remonstrated Miss Henderson.

"It 's no trouble whatever," Patty protested kindly. "I can take a cross cut, and meet you at the little summer-house where the boats are moored. It 's straight down this path; you can't miss it. Just follow that girl over there"; and she darted away.

The lecturer gazed dubiously after her a moment, and then started on after the girl, who cast a look over her shoulder and quickened, her pace. It was growing quite dusky under the trees, and the lecturer hurried on, trying to keep the girl in sight; but she unexpectedly turned a corner and disappeared, and at the same moment two strange girls suddenly dropped into the path, apparently from the tree-tops.

"Good evening," they said pleasantly. "Are you taking a walk?"

The lecturer started back with an exclamation of surprise; but as soon as she could regain her composure, she replied politely that she was strolling about and looking at the campus.

"Perhaps you would like to stroll with us?" they inquired.

"Thank you, you are very kind; but I have an engagement to row with one of the students."

Priscilla and Bonnie exchanged delighted glances. They had evidently caught a resourceful young person.

"Oh, no; it 's too late for a row. You might get malaria," Priscilla remonstrated. "Come and sit on the fence with us and admire the stars; it 's a lovely night."

The lecturer cast an alarmed glance toward the fence, which appeared to have an unusually narrow top rail. "You are very kind," she stammered, "but I really can't stop. The girl will be waiting."

"Who is the girl?" they inquired.

"I don't know that I remember her name."

"Mildred Connaught?" Bonnie suggested.

"No; I don't think that is it, but I really can't say. I have only just met her."

Miss Henderson was growing more and more puzzled. In her day the students had not been in the habit of way-laying strangers with invitations to go walking and sit on fences.

"Ah, do stay with us," Bonnie begged, laying a hand on her arm. "We 're lonely and want some one to talk to—we 'll tell you a secret if you do."

"I am sorry," Miss Henderson murmured confusedly, "but—"

"We 'll tell you the secret anyway," said Bonnie, generously, "and I 'm sure you 'll be interested. The sophomores are going to have their tree ceremonies to-night!"

"And you know," Priscilla broke in, "that the freshmen really ought to attend them too—it does n't matter if they are n't invited. But where do you suppose the freshmen are to-night? They 're attending a foolish little lecture on the Roman Forum."

"And though we don't wish to seem insistent," Bonnie added, "we should really like to have your company until the lecture is over."

"Until the lecture is over! But I am the lecturer," gasped Miss Henderson.

Bonnie grinned delightedly. "I am happy to meet you," she said, with a bow. "And perhaps you do not recognize us. I am Mr. Sherlock Holmes, and this is my friend Dr. Watson."

Dr. Watson bowed, and remarked that it was an unexpected pleasure. He had often heard of the famous lecturer, but had never hoped to meet her.

Miss Henderson, who was not very conversant with recent literature, looked more dazed than ever. It flashed across her mind that there was an insane asylum in the neighborhood, and the thought was not reassuring.

"We 'll not handcuff you," said Bonnie, magnanimously, "if you 'll come with us quietly."

The lecturer, in spite of fervid protestations that she was a lecturer, presently found herself sitting on the fence, with a girl on either side grasping an elbow. A light was beginning to break upon her, together with a poignant realization of the fact that she was seeing more of the real college life than she cared for.

"What time is it?" she asked anxiously.

"Ten minutes past eight by my watch, but I think it 's a little slow," said Bonnie.

"I am afraid you 're going to be late for your lecture," said Priscilla. "It seems a pity to waste it. Suppose you tell it to us instead."

"Yes, do," urged Bonnie. "I just dote on the Roman Forum."

The lecturer preserved a dignified silence, which was broken only by the croaking of the frogs and the occasional remarks of the two detectives. She had relinquished all hope of ever seeing the Archæological Society, and had philosophically resigned herself to the prospect of sitting on the fence all night, when suddenly there burst out from across the campus a song of victory, mingled with cheers and inarticulate yells.

At the first sound, Bonnie and Priscilla tumbled down from the fence, bringing the lecturer with them, and, each grasping her by a hand, they started to run. "Come on and see the fun," they laughed. "You 're perfectly welcome; it 's no secret anymore." And, in spite of breathless protestations that she much preferred to walk, Miss Henderson found herself dashing across the campus in the direction of the sounds.

Heads suddenly appeared in the dormitory windows, doors banged, and girls came running from every quarter with excited exclamations: "The sophomores are having their tree ceremonies!" "Where are the freshmen?" "Why did n't they get there?"

A crowd quickly gathered in the shadow of the trees and watched the scene with laughing interest. A wide circle of colored lanterns swayed in the breeze, and, within, a line of white-robed figures wound and unwound about a tiny tree to the music of a solemn chant.

"Is n't it pretty? Are n't you glad we brought you?" Bonnie demanded as they pushed through the crowd.

The lecturer did not answer, for she caught sight of the Latin professor hurrying toward them.

"Miss Henderson! I was afraid you were lost. It is nearly half-past eight. The audience has been waiting, and we have been filling in the time with reports."

For a moment the lecturer was silent, being occupied with an amused scrutiny of the faces of her captors; and then she rose to the occasion like a lady and a scholar, and delivered a masterly apology, with never a reference to her sojourn on the fence.

Bonnie and Priscilla stared at each other without a word, and as Miss Henderson was led away to the remnants of her audience Patty suddenly appeared.

"Good evening, Mr. Sherlock Holmes and Dr. Watson. Did you solve your mystery?" she asked sweetly.

Priscilla turned her to the light and scrutinized her face.

Patty smiled back with wide-open, innocent eyes.

Priscilla knew the expression, and she shook her. "You little wretch!" she exclaimed.

Patty squirmed out from under her grasp. "If you remember," she murmured, "I once said that the Lick Observatory was in Dublin, Ireland. It was a very funny mistake, of course, but I know of others that are funnier."

"What do you mean?" Bonnie demanded.

"I mean," said Patty, "that I wish you never to mention the Lick Observatory again."

XV Patty and the Bishop

THE dressing-bell rang for Sunday morning service, and Patty laid down her book with a sigh and went and stood by the open window. The outside world was a shimmering green and yellow, the trees showed a feathery fringe against the sky, and the breeze was redolent of violets and fresh earth.

"Patty," called Priscilla, from her bedroom, "you 'll have to hurry if you want me to fasten your dress. I have to go to choir rehearsal."

Patty turned back with another sigh, and began slowly unhooking her collar. Then she sat down on the edge of the couch and stared absently out of the window.

A vigorous banging of bureau drawers in Priscilla's room was presently followed by Priscilla herself in the doorway. She surveyed her room-mate suspiciously. "Why are n't you dressing?" she demanded.

"I 'll fasten my own dress; you need n't wait," said Patty, without removing her eyes from the window.

"Bishop Copeley 's going to preach to-day, and he 's such an old dear; you must n't be late."

Patty elevated her chin a trifle and shrugged her shoulders.

"Are n't you going to chapel?"

Patty brought her gaze back from the window and looked up at Priscilla beseechingly. "It 's such a lovely day," she pleaded, "and I 'd so much rather spend the time out of doors; I 'm sure it would be a lot better for my spiritual welfare."

"It 's not a question of spiritual welfare; it 's a question of cuts. You 've already over-cut twice. What excuse do you intend to give when the Self-Government Committee asks for an explanation?"

I have just run away from you, Bishop Copeley

"'Sufficient unto the day,'" laughed Patty. "When the time comes I 'll think of a beautiful new excuse that will charm the committee."

"You ought to be ashamed to evade the rules the way you do."

"Where is the fun of living if you are going to make yourself a slave to all sorts of petty rules?" asked Patty, wearily.

"I don't know why you have a right to live outside of rules any more than the rest of us."

Patty shrugged. "I take the right, and every one else can do the same."

"Every one else can't," returned Priscilla, hotly, "for there would n't be any law left in college if they did. I should a good deal rather play out of doors myself than go to chapel, but I 've used up all my cuts and I can't. You could n't either if you had a shred of proper feeling left. The only way you can get out of it is by lying."

"Priscilla dear," Patty murmured, "people in polite society don't put things quite so baldly. If you would be respected in the best circles, you must practise the art of equivocation."

Priscilla frowned impatiently. "Are you coming, or are you not?" she demanded.

"I am not."

Priscilla closed the door–not quite as softly as a door should be closed–and Patty was left alone. She sat thinking a few minutes with slightly flushed cheeks, and then as the chapel bell rang she shook herself and laughed. Even had she wished to go it was too late now, and all feeling of responsibility vanished. As soon as the decorous swish of Sunday silks had ceased in the corridor outside, she caught up a book and a cushion, and, creeping down by the side stairs, set gaily out across the sunlit lawn, with the deliciously guilty thrill of a truant little boy who has run away from school.

From the open windows of the chapel she could hear the college chanting: "Lord, have mercy upon us, and incline our hearts to keep this law." She laughed happily to herself; she was not keeping laws to-day. They might stay in there in the gloom, if they wanted to, with their commandments and their litanies. She was worshiping under the blue sky, to the jubilant chanting of the birds.

She was the only person alive and out that morning, and the spring was in her blood, and she felt as though she owned the world. The campus had never seemed so radiant. She paused on the little rustic bridge to watch the excited swirling of the brook, and she nearly lost her balance while trying to launch a tiny boat made of a piece of bark. She dropped pebbles into the pool in order to watch the startled frogs splash back into the water, and she threw her cushion at a squirrel, and laughed aloud at its angry chattering. She raced up the side of Pine Bluff, and dropped down panting on the fragrant needles in the shadow of a tall pine.

Below her the ivy-covered buildings of the college lay clustered among the trees; and in the Sunday quiet, with the sunlight shining on the towers, it looked like some medieval village sleeping in the valley. Patty gazed down dreamily with half-shut eyes, and imagined that presently a band of troubadours and ladies would come riding out on milk-white mules. But the sight of Peters, strolling to the gateway in his Sunday clothes, spoiled the illusion, and she turned to her book with a smile. Presently she closed it, however. This was not the time for reading. One could read in winter and when it rained, and even in the college library with every one else turning pages; but out here in the open, with the real things of life happening all about, it was a waste of opportunity.

Her eyes wandered back to the campus again, and she suddenly grew sober as the thought swept over her that in a few weeks more it would be hers no longer. This happy, irresponsible community life, which had come to be the only natural way of living, was suddenly at an end. She remembered the first day of being a freshman, when everything but herself had looked so big, and she had thought desperately, "Four years of this!" It had seemed like an eternity; and now that it was over it seemed like a minute. She wanted to clutch the present and hold it fast. It was a terrible thing–this growing old.

And there were the girls. She would have to say good-by, with no opening day in the fall–and Priscilla lived in California and Georgie in South Dakota and Bonnie in Kentucky and she in New

England, and they were the only people in the world she particularly cared to talk to. She would have to get acquainted with her mother's friends–with chronically grown-up people, who talked about husbands and children and servants. And there would be men. She had never had time to know many men; but some day she would probably be marrying one of them, and then all would be over; and before she had time to think, she would be an old lady, telling her grandchildren stories about when she was a girl.

Patty gazed mournfully down on the campus, almost on the verge of tears over her lost youth, when a step suddenly sounded on the gravel path, and she looked up with a startled glance to see a churchly figure rounding the hill. Involuntarily she prepared for flight; but the bishop had spied her, together with a little rustic seat under a tree, and he smiled upon the one and dropped down upon the other with a sigh of content.

"A beautiful view," he gasped; "but a very steep hill."

"It is steep," Patty agreed politely; and as there seemed to be no chance of escape, she resumed her seat and added, with a laugh: "I have just run away from you, Bishop Copeley, and here you come following along behind like an accusing conscience."

The bishop chuckled. "I 've run away myself," he returned; "I knew I should have to be introduced to a hundred or so of you after service, so I just slipped out the back way for a quiet stroll."

Patty eyed him appreciatively, with a new sense of fellow-feeling.

"I should like to have run away from church as well," he confessed, with a twinkle in his eye. "Out of doors is the best church on a day like this."

"That 's what I think," said Patty, cordially; "but I had no idea that bishops were so sensible."

They chatted along in a friendly manner on various subjects, and exchanged lay opinions on the college and the clergy.

"It 's a funny thing about this place," said Patty, ruminatingly, "that, though we have a different preacher every Sunday, we always have the same sermon."

"The same sermon?" inquired the bishop, somewhat aghast.

"Practically the same," said Patty. "I 've heard it for four years, and I think I could almost preach it myself. They all seem to think, you know, that because we come to college we must be monsters of reason, and they urge us to remember that reason and science are not the only things that count in the world–that feeling is, after all, the main factor; and they quote a little poem about the flower being beautiful, I know not why. That was n't what yours was about?" she asked anxiously.

"Not this time," said the bishop; "I preached an old one."

"It 's the best way," said Patty. "We 're human beings, if we do come to college. I remember once we had a man from Yale or Harvard or some such place, and he preached an old sermon: he urged us to become more manly. It was very refreshing."

The bishop smiled. "Do you run away from church very often?" he inquired mildly.

"No; I don't have a chance when I room with Priscilla. But obligatory chapel makes you want to run away," she added. "It 's not the chapel I object to; it 's the obligatoriness."

"But you have a system of–er–cuts," he suggested.

"Three a month," said Patty, sadly. "Evening chapel counts as one, but Sunday morning church as two."

"So you expended two cuts to escape me?" he asked with a smile.

"Oh, it was n't you," Patty remonstrated hastily. "It was just–the obligatoriness. And besides," she added frankly, "my legitimate cuts were used up days ago, and when I once begin over-cutting, I am reckless."

"And may I ask what happens when you over-cut?" the bishop inquired.

"Well," said Patty, "there are proctors, you know, that mark you when you are absent; and then, if they find that you 've over-cut, the Self-Government Committee calls you up and asks the reason. If you can't produce a good excuse you are deprived of your privileges for a month, and you can't be on committees or in plays or get leave of absence to go out of town."

"I see," said the bishop; "and will you have to suffer all of those penalties?"

"Oh, no," said Patty, comfortably; "I shall produce a good excuse."

"What will you say?" he inquired.

"I don't know, exactly; I shall have to depend on the inspiration of the moment."

The bishop regarded her quizzically. "Do you mean," he asked, "that, having broken the rule, you intend to evade the penalty by–to put it flatly–a falsehood?"

"Oh, no, bishop," said Patty, in a shocked tone. "Of course I shall tell the truth, only"–she looked up in the bishop's face with an irresistible smile–"the committee probably won't understand it."

For an instant the bishop's face relaxed, and then he grew grave again. "By a subterfuge?" he asked.

"Y-yes," acknowledged Patty; "I suppose you might call it a subterfuge. I dare say I am pretty bad," she added, "but you have to have a reputation for something in a place like this or you get overlooked. I can't compete in goodness or in athletics or in anything like that, so there 's nothing left for me but to surpass in badness–I have quite a gift for it."

The corners of the bishop's mouth twitched. "You don't look like one with a criminal record."

"I 'm young yet," said Patty. "It has n't commenced to show."

"My dear little girl," said the bishop, "I have already preached one sermon to-day, which you did n't come to hear, and I can't undertake to preach another for your benefit,"–Patty looked relieved,–"but there is one question I should like to ask you. In after years, when you are through college and the question is asked of some of your class-mates, 'Did you know–' You have not told me your name."

"Patty Wyatt."

"'Did you know Patty Wyatt, and what sort of a girl was she?' will the answer be what you would wish?"

Patty considered. "Ye-yes; I think, on the whole, they 'd stand by me."

"This morning," the bishop continued placidly, "I asked a professor in an entirely casual way about a young woman–a class-mate of your own–who is the daughter of an old friend of mine. The answer was immediate and unhesitating, and you can imagine how much it gratified me. 'There is not a finer girl in college,' he replied. 'She is honest in work and honest in play, and thoroughly conscientious in everything she does.'"

"Um-m," said Patty; "that must have been Priscilla."

"No," smiled the bishop, "it was not Priscilla. The young woman of whom I am speaking is the president of your Student Association, Catherine Fair."

"Yes, it 's true," said Patty, critically. "Cathy Fair hits straight from the shoulder."

"And would n't you like to go out with that reputation?"

"I 'm really not very bad," pleaded Patty, "that is, as badness goes. But I could n't be as good as Cathy; it would be going against nature."

"I am afraid," suggested the bishop, "that you do not try very hard. You may not think that it matters what people think now that you are young, but how will it be when you grow older? And it will not be long," he added. "Age slips upon you before you realize it."

Patty looked sober.

"You will soon be thirty, and then forty, and then fifty."

Patty sighed.

"And do you think that a woman of that age is attractive if she deals in subterfuges and evasions?"

Patty squirmed a trifle, and dug a little hole in the pine-needles with her toe.

"You must remember that you cannot form your character in a moment, my dear. Character is a plant of slow growth, and the seeds must be planted early."

The bishop rose, and Patty scrambled to her feet with a look of relief. He took the pillow and the book under his arm, and they started down the hill. "I have preached you a sermon, after all," he said apologetically; "but preaching is my trade, and you must forgive an old man for being prosy."

Patty held out her hand with a smile as they stopped before the door of Phillips Hall. "Good-by, bishop," she said, "and thank you for the sermon; I guess I needed it–I am getting old."

She climbed the stairs slowly, and, hesitating a moment outside her own room, where the sound of laughing voices through the transom betokened that the clan was gathered, she kept on to the door of a single at the end of the corridor.

"Come in," a voice called in response to her knock.

Patty turned the knob and stuck her head in. "Hello, Cathy! Are you busy?"

"Of course not. Come in and talk to me."

Patty shut the door and leaned with her back against it. "This is n't a social call," she announced impressively. "I 've come to see you officially."

"Officially?"

"You 're president of students, I believe?"

"I believe I am," sighed Cathy; "and if the President of the United States has half as much trouble with his subjects as I have with mine, he has my sincerest sympathy."

"I suppose we are a great deal of trouble," said Patty, contritely.

"Trouble! My dear," said Cathy, solemnly. "I 've spent the entire week running around to the different cottages making speeches to those blessed freshmen. They won't hand in chapel excuses, and they will run off with library books, and, altogether, they 're an immoral lot."

"They can afford to be; they 're young," sighed Patty, enviously. "But I," she added, "am getting old, and it 's time I was getting good. I 've called to tell you that I 've over-cut four times, and I have n't any excuse."

"What are you talking about?" asked Cathy, in amazement.

"Chapel excuses. I 've over-cut four times,–I think it 's four, though I 've rather lost count,–and I have n't any excuse."

"But, Patty, don't tell me that. You must have some excuse, some reason for–"

"Not the shadow of one. Just stayed away because I did n't feel like going."

"But you must give me some reason," remonstrated Cathy, in distress, "or I 'll have to report it to the committee and you 'll be deprived of your privileges. You can't afford that, you know, for you 're chairman of the Senior Prom."

"But I did n't have any excuse, and I can't make one up," said Patty. "I will soon be thirty, and then forty, and then fifty. Do you think a woman of that age is attractive if she deals in subterfuges and evasions? Character," she added solemnly, "is a plant of slow growth, and the seeds must be planted early."

Cathy looked puzzled. "I don't know what you 're talking about," she said, "but I suppose you do. Anyway," she added, "I 'm sorry about the chairmanship; but I 'm–well, I 'm sort of glad, too." She laid a hand on Patty's shoulder. "Of course I 've always liked you, Patty,–everybody does,–but I don't believe I 've ever appreciated you, and I 'm glad to find it out before we leave college."

Patty's face flushed a trifle and she drew away half sheepishly. "You 'd best postpone your felicitations until to-morrow," she laughed, "for I may think of some good excuse in the night. Good-by."

She was greeted in the study with a cry of welcome.

"Well, Patty," said Priscilla, "I hear you 've been taking a walk with the bishop. Did you tell him you 'd cut chapel?"

"I did; and he said he wished he might have cut, too."

"She 's incorrigible," sighed Georgie; "she 's even been corrupting the bishop."

"You 'd better be careful, Patty Wyatt," warned Bonnie Connaught. "Self-Government will get you if you don't watch out, and then you 'll be sorry when they take you off the Senior Prom."

Patty sobered for a moment, but she hastily assumed a nonchalant air. "They have got me," she laughed, "and I 'm already off–or, at least, I shall be as soon as they have a meeting."

"Patty!" cried the room, in a horrified chorus. "What do you mean?"

Patty shrugged. "Just what I say: deprived of my privileges for cutting chapel."

"It 's a shame!" said Georgie, indignantly. "That Self-Government Committee is going a little too far when it takes a senior's privileges away without even hearing her case." She grasped Patty by the arm and started toward the door. "Come on and tell Cathy Fair about it. She will fix it all right."

Patty hung back and disengaged her wrist from Georgie's grasp. "Let me alone," she said sulkily. "There 's nothing to be done. I told her myself I had n't any excuse."

"You told her?" Georgie stared her incredulity, and Bonnie Connaught laughed.

"Patty reminds me of the burglar who crawled out the back window with the silver, and then rang the front door-bell and handed it back."

"What 's the matter, Patty?" Priscilla asked solicitously. "Don't you feel well?"

Patty sighed. "I 'm getting old," she said.

"You 're getting what?"

"Old. Soon I 'll be thirty, and then forty, and then fifty; and do you think any one will love me then if I deal in subterfuges and evasions? Character, my dear girls, is a plant of slow growth, and the seeds must be planted early."

"You went and told the committee voluntarily,–of your own accord,–without even waiting to be called up?" Georgie persisted, determined to get at the facts of the case.

"I 'm getting old," repeated Patty. "It 's time I was getting good. As I said before, character is a plant–"

Georgie looked at the others and shook her head in bewilderment, and Bonnie Connaught laughed and murmured to the room in general "When Patty gets to heaven I 'm afraid the Recording Angel will have some trouble in balancing his books."